SHERLOCK HOLMES
And
The Mystery of
Einstein's Daughter

by

Tim Symonds

1

Paperback ISBN 978-1-78092-572-1
ePub ISBN 978-1-78092-573-8
PDF ISBN 978-1-78092-574-5

Published in the UK by MX Publishing
335 Princess Park Manor, Royal Drive, London, N11 3GX

www.mxpublishing.com

Cover by www.staunch.com

Tim Symonds was born in London. He grew up in Somerset, Dorset and Guernsey. After several years working in the Kenya Highlands and along the Zambezi he emigrated to the United States. He studied at Göttingen and at the University of California, Los Angeles, where he graduated Phi Beta Kappa in Political Science.

He is a Fellow of the Royal Geographical Society.

Sherlock Holmes And The Mystery Of Einstein's Daughter was written in a converted oast house near Rudyard Kipling's old home, Bateman's in East Sussex and in the forests and hidden valleys of the High Weald. The plot is based on an original online research paper published by Tim Symonds, titled 'A Vital Detail In The Story Of Albert Einstein'.

The author's other detective novels include *Sherlock Holmes and The Case of the Bulgarian Codex* and *Sherlock Holmes and The Dead Boer at Scotney Castle.*

Britain's former Foreign Secretary, Sir Malcolm Rifkind emailed the author: 'Dear Tim Symonds, just to say that I have just finished reading *The Dead Boer at Scotney Castle*. I greatly enjoyed it and found it a great yarn! It kept one guessing right to the end, which all good crime novels should do. Sherlock Holmes (and Conan Doyle) would have been impressed!'

And on Nick Cardillo's blogspot (The Consulting Detective): *Sherlock Holmes And The Mystery of Einstein's Daughter* is Tim Symonds' third Sherlock Holmes pastiche, the other two I have yet to read, but if they are like this they should make some interesting reading. The author's research into his subjects is terrific, weaving in Sherlockian and historical knowledge into the plot. Reading *Einstein's Daughter* was not only presenting a fine mystery, but a learning experience and a fine showcase into the situation of turn-of-the-century Europe.'

http://the-consulting-detective.blogspot.com/2014/03/review-holmes-and-mystery-of-einstein.html)

Foreword

Albert Einstein was born in the Swabian town of Ulm and grew up in Munich, a bustling, wealthy town in southern Germany. At the age of five he was shown how a compass needle always swings to magnetic North. From that moment Albert determined to become a great physicist, more famous even than Isaac Newton. History shows he succeeded – beyond even his own wildest boyhood dreams - but an event occurred during his student days at the Zurich Polytechnikum which could have brought his ambitions to a juddering halt.

When Einstein applies for a post as Lecturer at Berne University, the Head of the Physics Department asks Sherlock Holmes to search out for any skeletons in the young man's cupboard. The unexpected request takes Holmes and Watson deep into the Serbia of 1905, into one of the most perplexing mysteries they had ever encountered.

Tim Symonds

Springtime 2014

To LJA

Preliminaries

by

Dr. John H. Watson

The events I relate in *The Mystery of Einstein's Daughter* took place well into the beneficent reign of King Edward the Seventh, the year in which the Simplon Tunnel was driven through the Alps and when Charles Perrine discovered Jupiter's seventh satellite, Elara. In faraway South Africa, Thomas Evan Powell brought the Cullinan, the world's largest rough diamond, to the surface. In England there was talk of a new automobile association employing cycle scouts to help unwary motorists avoid police speed traps.

In the spring of that year, my comrade Sherlock Holmes undertook an investigation into what at first appeared to be a very inconsequential matter concerning a recent graduate of the Physics Department of a Swiss *Polytechnikum*. It turned out not to be so humdrum a matter after all. The young man's name was Albert Einstein. He was soon to become the world's most revered scientist, gaining fame and respect the equal of, or greater than, Presidents and Prime Ministers.

Dr John H. Watson
Junior United Service Club
London

Contents

CHAPTER I

Watson is Offered a Commission

Early in 1905 the *Strand Magazine*'s Publisher, Sir George Newnes, approached me with an offer: would I accept the kingly sum of six hundred guineas in return for securing a photograph of my comrade-in-arms Sherlock Holmes at the now-infamous Reichenbach Falls in the Bernese Oberland? Sir George wanted an engraving or half-tone illustration from the plate to grace the *Strand*'s Christmas cover. The Falls were the site of the death of the arch-criminal Professor Moriarty at the great detective's hands fourteen years earlier, on 4 May 1891. Six hundred guineas was the equal of three years of my Army half-pay pension, hard-earned in the arid Pāriyātra Parvata and a pestilential stint at the Rawal Pindi Base hospital, both of which I deemed myself lucky to have survived.

'A front-cover picture of Sherlock Holmes at the Reichenbach Falls will increase the run by at least a quarter of a million,' Sir George opined gleefully.

He was right. A cover reprising Holmes's miraculous escape from a watery grave at Moriarty's hands would generate a welcome boost to sales.

Until his reappearance some three years later, it was believed that my great comrade had died in the struggle with Moriarty. During this Great Hiatus the obscure mountain stream and waterfall soon became a place of pilgrimage. The nearby Englischer Hof guest book was filled with guests' comments, keen to pay their respects. Visitors included the New York

Police Department alongside a delegation from the French *Sûreté* led by Monsieur Dubuque, and James McParland of the Pinkerton National Detective Agency. Troupes of young London City men and members of the burgeoning Sherlock Holmes societies travelled to the Falls in charabanc loads, wearing bands of black *crêpe* around their bowlers. Gaggles of women dressed in long grey travelling cloaks clustered at the cliff edge, staring silently down. Some cast a facsimile of Holmes's fore-and-aft cap (on sale at the local hotels) into the roiling waters below. The suicide watch at the cliff edge, normally posted for forlorn young lovers, now looked out for lone figures of distraught men and women ready to throw themselves into the chasm after the man they called 'the Master'.

The *Strand* would pay all costs for a journey retracing our original route. Holmes and I would tread once more in the footsteps of Goethe, Tolstoy and Nietzsche along the charming Rhone Valley. Sir George wanted the photograph to show Holmes standing on the lip of the chasm, down which Moriarty tumbled (or rather, had been tumbled) to his end. The photograph was to capture the atmosphere of Jacques-Louis David's 'Napoleon At The Saint-Bernard Pass' – as Bonaparte himself put it, '*Calme sur un cheval fougueux*'. In the picture, Sherlock Holmes should stare down on the torrent, behind him crags piled one upon the other. My publisher looked at me quizzically. Did I think Holmes could be persuaded to strike a chord on his violin, staring down over the precipice as though viewing Moriarty's body cannonading from rock to jutting rock? I replied that it was a ludicrous idea. The spray from the rushing torrent would badly upset a Stradivarius.

My publisher's wish for an exclusive front-cover to boost sales was understandable. The publishing business was becoming highly-competitive. The daily journey to work for large numbers of the population had triggered a demand for reading material from newspapers such as the *Daily Mail* and magazines with short articles and stories. Titles like the *Harmsworth Magazine* or *Pearson's Magazine* offered articles of scientific and historical interest, cartoons and celebrity gossip. The *Strand* looked over its shoulder at the rapid growth of a particularly vulgar halfpenny dreadful, the Penny Blood *Union Jack* magazine, popular with young men. The *Union Jack's* circulation had been lifted by the adventures of the upstart detective Sexton Blake, the poor man's Sherlock Holmes, and his scent hound Pedro. Another rival was Hornung's disgraceful invention, A. J. Raffles, the 'gentleman thief', whose criminal exploits promoted the sales of *Cassell's Magazine*.

***

In the early stages of the Great Hiatus I was approached only once for assistance by Lestrade, the ferret-like Scotland Yard Inspector. On this occasion, through my medical knowledge, I was instrumental in solving a crime dubbed by the *Evening Standard*, 'The Case of The Ghost of Grosvenor Square', a sobriquet picked up and parodied by *Punch*.

After Holmes's assumed death, I welcomed an invitation from his brother Mycroft to return to Baker Street, to put my former comrade's papers and possessions in order. Tears had sprung to my eyes when I looked at a lifetime's souvenirs – the Yupik wolf mask sent from a shaman in Nunivak in 1890, a huge barbed-headed spear, a carving of the demi-god Maui, Lombardini's *Antonio Stradivari e la celebre scuola cremonese*, the tennis rackets and cricket gear Holmes last employed in his short time at university.

I relocated the most precious of these household gods and books from the sitting room to his bedroom, which became for me as great a shrine as the bedroom of the late admired Prince Albert in Queen Victoria's eyes. I left three physical reminders of my friend's still palpable presence centre-stage on the deal-top breakfast table. The violin, with its well-flamed maple, fine belly grain, and orangey brown varnish glowed where it lay in the morning sun. At its side the bow, like the bayonet of a fallen soldier. And his pipe-rack.

Upon Holmes's miraculous reappearance, Mrs. Hudson and I had hauled the books back, together with the Betjemann Tantalus, the basket chair, the Persian slipper containing his tobacco (freshly restocked), the writing-desk, bear-skin rug, and a gasogene given to bursting. One wall remained bejewelled with fine fragments of glass shrapnel from such an explosion until we ordered an extensive refurbishment of the front room.

It was not long after his return that Holmes once again showed his talent for the unexpected. He announced his retirement. I was to read it on the front page of *The Daily Express* and beneath a dramatic headline on the third page of *The Times*. My old comrade expressed his long-standing desire – completely unsuspected by me – to give himself up entirely 'to that soothing life of Nature'. I was as astonished as if I had opened the newspapers that day to find his obituary ('Once again the world mourns the passing of the great Consulting Detective Mr. Sherlock Holmes...').

Holmes told reporters he wanted to enter upon a quiet and congenial existence in Sussex with his Italian bees, *Apis mellifera ligustica*, a mild subspecies of the western honey bee. Holmes's first effort with a particularly aggressive black bee with yellowish bands on the sides of the abdomen had brought a delegation of shepherds to his door, demanding their extinction or at least removal to the neighbouring county of Kent. A *Punch* caricaturist attempted an explanation for Sherlock Holmes's retirement. Under the caption 'The Old Horse has pulled *a Heavy Load* a Long Way', Holmes was portrayed as a preternaturally elderly nag drawing a cart piled high with my chronicles (my head showing through).

The announcement of Holmes's retirement hit me like the blast of a Fenian bomb. I had taken it for granted that I was a south wind in Holmes's life, like the old black clay pipe, or the Stradivarius, or the shag tobacco with its tendency to stain the inner surfaces of his teeth. The prospect of imminent separation shocked me deeply. It made no sense. Holmes was at the very height of his powers. In the world of crime detection he was *Facile princeps*. He was hardly 49 years of age.

I confronted my old friend and he confirmed his decision to turn his hand to beekeeping at his Sussex farmstead. This was not the man I knew. Just as the green anaconda finds the Brazilian jungle its natural home and slithers not a jot beyond its boundaries, London was Holmes's favoured haunt, not an old farmhouse tucked against a line of trees to withstand the full-frontal winter gales blasting in from the English Channel. The Sherlock Holmes I knew was addicted to the ever-changing kaleidoscope of life, ebbing and flowing through Trafalgar Square, or Pickle Herring Street with its line of small shipping offices. It was to the busy hum of men amid the sounds and sights of Hansom cabs, wing collars and flickering gas-light that Holmes went for recreation and inspiration. Whenever I waxed lyrical over the beauty of the English countryside (being a countryman by birth), Holmes had not been notably moved.

I have reported Holmes's life-long attitude towards country life in *The Adventure of the Copper Beeches*:

All over the countryside, away to the rolling hills around Aldershot, the little red and grey roofs of the farmsteads peeped out from amid the light green of the new foliage.

'Are they not fresh and beautiful?' I cried with all the enthusiasm of a man fresh from the fogs of Baker Street.

But Holmes shook his head gravely.

'Do you know, Watson,' said he, 'that it is one of the curses of a mind with a turn like mine that I must look at everything with reference to my own special subject. You look at these scattered houses, and you are impressed by their beauty. I look at them, and the only thought which comes to me is a feeling of their isolation and of the impunity with which crime may be committed there.'

Now, suddenly, London – and I – found ourselves alone, without him.

CHAPTER II

Back Together in Baker Street

Sir George's commission was an intriguing opportunity to rebuild my former warm relationship with Holmes. A return to the Reichenbach Falls would be like old times. I would seat myself opposite him aboard an ultra-quick *locomotive à bec*, service revolver in my coat pocket, the thrill of adventure in my heart. Once more we would cross the Gemmi Pass, our goal Interlaken or at least Daubensee, for a good night's rest in the fresh mountain air. Then, fifteen miles beyond, to the small village of Meiringen, a refuge in the wild and romantic landscape of the Rosenlaui valley, within close hiking distance of our goal. Sir George had made me an attractive and, at six hundred guineas, a remunerative offer, but how was I to persuade Holmes to agree? Yuletide and the irregular week-end visit to Sussex to bring him up-to-date with the London gossip was the most I saw of him.

At the start of spring the opportunity presented itself to meet up with Holmes at our old Baker Street abode, which he had kept on for occasional trips to London. It was occasioned by his need to repair the storm-damaged roof of his farmhouse. For a fleeting period we could again inhabit the site of our old adventures. The Capital's winter fogs were dispersing under the gathering warmth. Munificent daffodil harvests from distant Guernsey and Devon tumbled into Paddington for the Covent Garden flower market, a hundred boxes at a time. The Banjo barometer hanging in the hallway at 221B, Baker Street – the jewel in our landlady Mrs. Hudson's possessions – seldom dipped below 30 inches. We put away the bitter cold of winter such as I had encountered at Holmes's farm on the close-cropped turf and rusting quiet of the Sussex Downs. To recline on his veranda between October and May, admiring a distant view of the English Channel, required the fortitude of Scott of the Antarctic.

I was happy once more to exchange medicine for biography. I had recalled the faithful Anstruther to manage my practice in my absence. But there was a problem. The plan was not proceeding as I had hoped. Holmes seemed to be passing through an unusually serene period. Most mornings after our return to Baker Street, he rose late, lit up the first pipe of the day and settled himself in his chair. The breakfast things, their work done, awaited removal – a tub of Burgess's Genuine Anchovy Paste, a packet of Pall Mall Turkish cigarettes and an empty toast-rack. What of new adventures? Each day my comrade turned to his notes for a work long in gestation (which his admirers await to this day), a textbook he claimed would 'focus the whole art of detection' into a single volume. An hour or so later he would reach for the commonplace book which I flatter with the title 'Great Index' to continue catching up on two years' cross-referencing. To keep up-to-date with additions and losses and changes of residence required perpetual pasting of newspaper clippings. The Index contained notes on cases which interested him, many transcribed from the crime pages of the *Daily Telegraph* or recent editions of *Criminals of Europe and America*. Under 'A', Holmes recorded the machinations of Irene Adler, the New Jersey-born contralto. She was sandwiched between an affable Hebrew Rabbi named Hermann Adler and a staff-commander who had written a monograph on deep-sea fishes.

By noon, Holmes would tire of cross-referencing and exchange the Great Index for the acid-charred bench of chemicals, dipping into this or that bottle, drawing out a few drops of each with his glass pipette. Well into the night he tinkered with apparatus the equal of a well-stocked university laboratory – Leyden jars, Liebig condensers, watch glasses, evaporation dishes. Pungent gases filled the room and began a slow march out into the landing. Every so often he would emit an explosive guffaw of delight like the cork popping from a bottle of champagne. I presumed he was working on yet another ordeal poison to add to the West African devil's-foot root (*radix pedis diaboli*).

He spent one entire day on the sofa browsing through *Out Of Doors*, a little chocolate and silver volume by the famous observer J.C. Wood. I had become accustomed to living with equanimity on the slopes of a volcano but the atmosphere of violence and danger which hung around him was dissipating fast. Could the indolent man before me be the same person I quoted in *The Adventure of Wisteria Lodge*, whose mind was 'tearing itself to pieces' because it was not connected up to the work for which it was built? In busier times the front-door bell or telephone would ring many times in the day. Not now. Where were the visiting cards, their texture, style of engraving, even the hour of delivery able to convey a subtle and unmistakable intelligence? Noting my boredom Holmes murmured, 'Watson, my dear friend, the lion isn't always on the hunt'.

Despite the arrival of the daffodils and the cyan skies, my thoughts were far from spring-like. A month earlier, a Neal

Cannetty had arrived to take me to lunch at The Criterion. An envoy from Norman Hapgood, the Editor of *Collier's, The National Weekly*, he was on a mission. His grating obsequiousness reminded me of Dickens's oleaginous character Uriah Heep. We worked our way through a delightful *consommé de gibier*, followed by lamb cutlets. A dessert of *Charlotte russe*, with its ratafia-soaked sponge fingers, was accompanied by dollops of flattery as rich as the dish itself.

Replete, my host sat back. In a tone similar to my bank manager's (and the equal in insincerity), Cannetty assured me for his part, it was a pleasure to meet me. The American Editor had nothing particular in mind. There was just one thing. My chronicles (while remarkably pleased as the Editor was with them) would benefit from a tiny embellishment.

'A tiny embellishment?' I returned.

Cannetty's lips fluttered in his corpulent face like the Scarlet Peacock butterfly of Trinidad and Tobago. He nodded.

'A small embellishment, yes.'

'On the matter of – ?'

'Corpses.'

The American readership was complaining. Dead bodies made an appearance in hardly more than one-in-three of my chronicles. So sparingly did I dole out the victims that in *Sherlock Holmes And The Case of the Dead Boer At Scotney Castle* the corpse didn't put in an appearance until Page 72. Worse still, it was the only death in the plot. To put it bluntly, Mr. Cannetty told me, there were not enough dead colonels with ivory paper knives thrust into their midriffs to fill the ice-boxes of a small country coroner in Alabama. Couldn't I make London's East End a little more exotic? Bring in some dacoits and Thuggees? In short, couldn't I make my deathless stories a little less *deathless*?

I agreed with him. It was a problem. Nevertheless, the scarcity of corpses in English villas or upon distant moors could hardly be laid at the feet of Mr. Sherlock Holmes. I apologised volubly for the undeniable fact: there had indeed been of late be a most unfortunate dearth of murders, dating back almost to the day in 1901 when Edward became King. England herself needed to buck up and do better. The hangman and Old Bailey judges were being put out of work. Even the Home Secretary was upset. The Whitechapel murders were now, alas, a distant memory. Would America like to send us some gun-toting villains surplus to Chicago's requirements and let them loose on London's theatre district?

I finished working my way through a second helping of the *Charlotte russe* and threw my napkin down on the table. Besides, I said, I too had a bone to pick. I disliked his employer's habit of corrupting my chronicles with unauthorised changes, inexplicable omissions and transpositions of letters and words. And, most of all, switching weather in contradiction to records in *The Times*.

***

My thoughts returned to Holmes. I racked my brains. What could I do to gain his consent to a photograph at the exact spot where he threw his greatest foe to his death? Unwisely, I had taken the *Strand* publisher's proffered advance of a hundred guineas without first broaching the matter with the subject of the proposed photograph. The advance had evaporated like haze

21

before a tropical sun. The twenty-one £5 notes had been put to good use, settling my tabs at the Junior United Service Club.

For many years, Holmes had resisted any return to the Reichenbach Falls. When I mooted the idea some five years earlier Holmes responded tersely, 'You must drop it, Watson; you really must, you know'. On another occasion Madame Tussaud's offered Holmes a substantial sum to advise on Moriarty's wax portrait. It would portray the look of horror on the arch-criminal's face as he slipped over the cliff edge to his doom, one hand reaching up like a vulture clawing at the sky. The commission was rejected out of hand.

I was at a loss for a ruse to lure Holmes back to the Falls. The matter was complicated by a not-especially attractive attribute Holmes shared with the Ottoman Turk. From the moment his ears picked up the word 'no' falling from his own lips it seemed nothing in the world, neither convention nor friendship would oblige him to retract it. Like the chameleon fixating its prey, I stared at him as he stooped over his latest chemical experiment. He stood sideways to me, attired in his mouse-coloured dressing-gown. Sherlock Holmes's physiognomy at rest has been compared to the famed Red Indian chief Sitting Bull. My recent visit to the Bristol City Museum's Assyrian and Egyptian mummy gallery showed how remarkably similar he was in profile to Horemkenesi, the Egyptian 11th Century B.C. priest and official.

My gaze switched to the cold joint of beef on our sideboard left by our kindly landlady to ensure Holmes did not go hungry through an arduous chemical night. Letters which he at some point planned to answer were pinned down by a jack-knife on the mantel-shelf. One letter was from a Miss Julia Freeman, captain of the Glynde Butterflies Stoolball team. Would Holmes come to Lewes to umpire the final match of the season against the formidable Chailey Grasshoppers? The Great Western Railway begged permission to name their newest locomotive after Holmes. Another invited him to address the Three Hours for Lunch Club, the event in question set for some weeks past. A sudden emission of a vile gas from an over-heated boiling tube sent my companion gasping backwards. A flying hand knocked the microscope to the floor. Still choking, Holmes retreated from the chemical corner towards the half-open window. He flung it wide to encourage an exchange of our gas-laden atmosphere with the slightly less fetid air of Baker Street.

If Holmes could be persuaded to return to the Falls, photographic equipment would pose no problem. Readers of *The Case Of The Bulgarian Codex* will recall how the Prince Regnant of Bulgaria presented me with a mahogany Sanderson Bellows camera in Sofia in 1900. I had left it behind in our Baker Street lodgings in the move to my new practice in West Kensington. The magnificent creation still stood in prime place in a corner of our sitting-room. Professional photographers were turning to smaller cameras, especially roll-film models. I intended to stay with my older, trusted, wooden Sanderson though I had been tempted by the sight of a brass-bound Meagher among the pages of advertisements in the *Strand* for Rowlands' Kalydor ('Cools and refreshes the face and arms of Ladies, and all exposed to the Hot Sun and Dust'), and tins of Abdulla's Egyptian Tobacco Mix.

I stared affectionately at the Sanderson. It almost vibrated in anticipation of a visit to the Alps. All it needed was a trip to the photographic specialists to replace the focusing screen and check the bellows. Throw in a box of unexposed Paget plates and the commission was tantalisingly within my grasp, yet – unless I could come up with some inducement to persuade Holmes – desperately distant.

For a good while I sat by a fire still aglow from the previous night, the tiny flames flickering across the sea-coals. My comrade abandoned work with test-tubes and retorts and leant at the open window. He held the lace curtain aside, looking languidly down at the street. I reached across to the day's first edition of *The Times*. The inside pages briefly reported a terrible shoe factory disaster in Massachusetts. An exploding boiler caused the four-storey wooden building to collapse. Elsewhere, plans were afoot to celebrate the centenary of the Battle of Trafalgar. J.M.W. Turner's fine painting of the 98-gun ship 'Temeraire' would take centre stage at the National Gallery.

A headline caught my eye: 'DISCOVERER OF THE FIRST PYGMY HIPPOPOTAMI KNOWN TO SCIENCE VISITS THE REGENT'S PARK HEADQUARTERS OF THE ZOOLOGICAL SOCIETY OF LONDON'. The article continued:

This afternoon at three o'clock Dr. Johann Büttikofer, Director of the Zoological Garden at Rotterdam, will present a public lecture on discoveries made during his explorations of the Liberia interior in 1879-1882 and 1886-1887. Dr. Büttikofer collected the first complete specimens known to science of the pygmy hippopotamus, now at the Natural History Museum of Leiden. In recognition of this signal achievement, Switzerland's largest university, the University of

Berne, awarded Dr. Büttikofer a dr. h.c. in Natural Sciences.

'An Honorary Doctorate!' I exclaimed under my breath. 'Of course! That might do it!' With as casual an air as I could muster I said, 'I feel in need of fresh air. I'll take a short walk in Regent's Park.'

'Will you indeed?' came the response. 'I had no idea you were interested in the pygmy hippopotamus.'

'Why, how on – ?'

Holmes spluttered with laughter, pleased at my astonishment. 'You confess yourself utterly taken aback, Watson?'

'I do,' I admitted.

'My reasoning was simple enough. You are not interested in the Shipping News. You turn to the inside pages. You skim over the foiled attempt to steal the original manuscript of Dickens's *Great Expectations*. You alight on a small piece on wife-beating and move on to a report about the murder of two shopkeepers in south London, solved by the use of fingerprinting technique – I have long said that fingerprinting is almost as good as footprints. Finally you fixate on the fifth column of the page, towards the bottom. Now you remove your venerable hunter from the left pocket of your waistcoat, but you distrust the time it offers. You raise your head and stare hard at our grandfather clock. With surprising agility for a man of your age and condition, you leap to your feet.'

Holmes pointed at the newspaper in my hand. 'Only one article inside to-day's *Times* referred to an event taking place at a specific hour this afternoon, namely a lecture at the Regent's

Park Zoo at three o'clock. Indeed you must hurry, Watson. It's already a quarter past two.'

'My dear Holmes,' I protested, 'it's hardly a surprise that a lecture on exotic creatures attracts my interest. During my time in Gilgit-Baltistan I was considered an expert on the species of wild goat known as the markhor.'

On this immodest note I took my hat and made a hurried exit. Within minutes I was in the Regent's Park, crossing Clarence Bridge, and on towards the Zoo, passing lines of nannies seated in the shade of vast old horse-chestnuts while their charges played around them. The sun's light filtered down on the pages through the striking white upright inflorescences typical of the species. It was impossible to enter the Park on a fresh spring morning without a song in one's heart.

It was my fervent hope that an offer of an Honorary Doctorate from a Swiss university would tickle my comrade's fancy – and so draw us back to the Bernese Oberland, the site of the Reichenbach Falls. At the end of the lecture I approached our speaker, Dr. Büttikofer. An admirer of Sherlock Holmes's work, he readily agreed to contact the Rector at Berne University.

CHAPTER III

Holmes Receives the Offer of a Doctorate

I saw little of Holmes over the next few days. He was out when the post brought a large envelope stamped *Universitas Bernensis*. I eased the flap open. Dr. Büttikofer had done his job well. It contained the offer of an Honorary Doctorate contingent on Holmes's acceptance. I resealed the envelope and quit my breakfast before the marmalade stage.

On my return, Holmes was reading the invitation from Berne University. He looked pleased. 'I'm to be awarded a Doctorate *Honoris Causa*, Watson.'

He replaced the invitation in the envelope and added it to the pile of letters impaled on the mantelpiece. I was to accept on his behalf. Relief flooded through me. We would return to Switzerland. We would be within striking distance of the Reichenbach Falls, one step closer to the 600 guineas.

'Will you contact Mycroft before we leave for Berne?' I enquired. 'After all, if we are to encounter any difficulty abroad – '

Seven years the elder, Holmes's brother Mycroft held an indeterminate but unique position at the heart of Government. My comrade had described it thus: 'Occasionally Mycroft *is* the British government – the most indispensable man in the country. The conclusions of every department are passed to him. He is the central exchange, the clearinghouse. All other men are specialists, but his specialism is omniscience.'

'No, my dear friend, I suggest we keep this visit private,' came the firm reply. 'You recall our adventures in the Balkans five years ago. If we were to contact my brother we would once more find ourselves kow-towing to Royalty or engaging in High Politics.'

I sent off Holmes's acceptance at the Wigmore Street Post Office. On my return I found him seated in his basket chair, his lap piled up with newspapers, topped by the *St. James's Gazette*. The dressing-gown indicated he was settling in for the rest of the day. On the small table lay a recent edition of *The Newspaper Press Directory and Advertiser's Guide*. Something was clearly being planned. Before I could enquire, he put aside the *Gazette*.

'Watson,' Holmes began, 'it must enter your mind that each time we leave these shores we put ourselves at ever-greater risk. I remind you, somewhere out there, waiting with bitter patience, lurks a vile and enterprising enemy.'

It was a subject I had hoped to avoid. I replied with a calmness I did not feel, 'I presume you are talking about our brush with Colonel Moran?'

This had been the very considerable brush I described in *The Adventure of the Empty House*. Holmes and I rated Colonel Sebastian Moran the most dangerous of our living foes. Hardly an Indian hill station household lacked a tiger-skin carpet displaying a single puncture from a Moran bullet. He was the son of a Minister to Persia, captain of the Eton College cricket Eleven when the peerless Ed Smith (later captain of Cambridge and author of *Luck*) was opening bat. Moran had embarked on a military career, serving in the Jowaki Expedition against the Afridis in 1877. After an involvement in the Second Anglo-Afghan War, Moran turned to the bad. Under a cloud, he returned to London to become chief of staff to the malevolent organising genius, Professor Moriarty.

'Why should Moran leave himself open to destruction by tackling you again?' I demanded. 'Surely he has learnt his lesson? He spends his time replenishing the pelf he lost on Moriarty's death. He makes very satisfactory sums at the tables of the rich and gullible in every gaming-house in London. Besides, there is no need for Moran to know about our trip. We shall take every precaution to keep our departure secret.'

'Watson,' came the reply, 'if you read the criminal news in to-day's newspapers, you will discover why Moran – like the wounded tiger he pursued down a drainpipe – may become doubly-dangerous. A return to Switzerland will be as perilous an undertaking as any we have ever faced together.'

Holmes pointed to the pile of newspapers. 'The Colonel is accused of cheating at cards. His favourite London gambling dens are considering expelling him. Moran will be declared *persona non grata* at every club in London. It will give him time to spare. He'll become doubly vengeful. I may have dodged death that day at the great Falls but one day our luck could run out.'

I asked, my voice a croak, 'You have had second thoughts about visiting Switzerland, Holmes? You now wish to refuse the Doctorate?' The trip to Berne was an essential step towards the photograph on which my financial well-being had now become heavily dependent.

'Not at all, Watson. I've accepted and we shall go. I merely stipulate one condition.'

'Name it,' I responded with relief.

'We must resort to artful disguise. For all your attendances at the London theatres, you have learnt very little of use in our present situation. Actors confront their audiences at a determined distance. Stage lighting creates illusion and effect. By contrast we ordinary mortals are at the mercy of the close encounter, the glare of the sun, the street-lamp or the torch.'

'I shall consider such preparation a privilege indeed, Holmes,' I replied, seating myself beside him. 'Instruction from the master himself.'

'Pick a disguise for yourself. What shall it be?'

'I've been re-reading Conrad's *Heart of Darkness*. I fancy myself as a retired captain of a river-steamboat who spent his life trading guns and ivory up and down the Congo River. Your own disguise as a respectable master mariner fallen into years of poverty is rated highly among the criminal underworld. The great painter J.M.W. Turner himself travelled through the Alps with his sketchbook, looking like the mate of a ship.'

Holmes replied drily, 'One wonders how many people other than Turner disguise themselves as retired master mariners and wander the Alps.'

'Nevertheless...' I began.

Holmes pressed his thin hands together. 'Dear Watson, you appear to consider it done if you emulate the decorator crab, covering its back with seaweed, sponges and stones. Slap on a captain's hat, add a coarse brown tint, adopt the rolling gait of the seafarer, speak like Long John Silver and complete the picture with Captain Flint upon a shoulder, squawking foul oaths in a Devonian accent. What if we happen across a retired captain of just such a river-boat? Think how large a part chance has played already in our little adventures. You may well be able to compare the antics of the Timurids to the Congo pygmies, but what if he finds you confused over whether river-boats measure their journeys in nautical or statute miles?'

'Surely river-boats use nautical miles like their sisters on the High Seas?' I replied.

'Unfortunately you're wrong, Watson. River-boats tend to use statute miles.'

My face fell. The sea-captain masquerade had suffered a leak.

With a cruel smile, Holmes continued. 'What if he asks you to share your knowledge of astronomical navigation and celestial geometry?'

Holed below the waterline, I abandoned a sea-captain's disguise.

'Let's start at first principles,' my comrade commenced. 'Whatever your camouflage, it must be tailored to the moment of maximum danger. Animals are readied by Nature - the coat of an African gazelle when it approaches the waterhole at dusk, darkest on those parts which tend to be most illuminated in the diminishing light. For Man, it is the battledress of a modern soldier. Luckily, Watson, Nature and your ancestors have bestowed upon you the perfect disguise. You have no need to add cryptic colouration to blend in with your habitat. You were born with it. With your features and your customary dress you could stand for an hour at Piccadilly Circus amid the throng, and not one person in a thousand would take any note of you. There is absolutely nothing *to* note about you. We need only give you a profession.'

He fixed me with a friendly look. 'You will need to mind your mannerisms, my friend. When we settle on whichever outfit, I implore you to keep to the minimum your irritating habit of drumming a tattoo on your knee with your notably fat fingers.'

'I'll do my best, Holmes,' I retorted, hurt.

***

The next day I breakfasted alone after a restless night. I could wait no longer. It was time to grasp the nettle. I left Holmes a note. Given we would be in the Bernese Oberland and in striking distance of the Reichenbach Falls, would he consent to a photograph for the *Strand*, the Christmas edition? A commission of six hundred guineas was on offer. I confessed I had already spent a hundred guineas up front. I grabbed my hat and hurried from our lodgings. Some hours later I returned, sick with trepidation. Holmes greeted me cordially.

'Good day, Watson,' he offered.

'Good day to you too, Holmes,' I responded anxiously. My note, now open, still lay among the uncleared dishes.

'Isn't it a wonderful time of the year!' my comrade went on. 'See how our plane tree contemplates unfurling its leathery – '

'Holmes!' I intervened, with an admonishing look.

He pointed through our window at the sky.

'And the moon at this time of the year! Even by day, see how clearly the mountains…'

'Holmes!' I yelped, 'for Heaven's sake!'

He dropped his arm and peered at me.

'Was there something you wanted to discuss? I seem to remember – now, what was it?'

'Your decision, Holmes, your decision!' I cried, pointing at the breakfast table.

He went to the Sanderson camera and posed by it, chuckling. 'I've decided to go along with your wishes, Watson. However, I have a further condition,' he said in a serious tone. 'We must cut and run if Colonel Moran discovers our enterprise. I have no intention of helping you shake hands with St. Peter so far ahead of your natural term. The terrain around the Falls could not be better designed for a master assassin with a telescopic sight. Other than your cumbrous service revolver, we shall be armed only with my Penang Lawyer.'

'You appear to have given this some thought, Holmes,' I replied. 'Do you have a plan to forestall Moran? '

'I do,' he affirmed. 'As he has time on his hands I think the Colonel should pay a visit to Ceylon.'

'Ceylon?' I exclaimed.

'As a matter of health.'

I gawped. The Crown Colony was not famed for its health-giving properties. Filarial diseases had spread throughout the Island of Ceylon as far back as the invasions of the Kalinga kings in the twelfth and thirteenth centuries.

'For his *health*?' I exclaimed, astonished.

'Not *his* health, Watson. Ours.'

'And how to you propose to accomplish that, may I ask? What if our Colonel doesn't want to visit Ceylon?'

Holmes replied, 'We shall offer ourselves as bait like the naked ankle to the malarial mosquito.' He picked up the old clay pipe he dubbed his 'counsellor'.

'We shall insert a 6-liner in the newspapers.'

The cost of inserting an advertisement in the principal papers was not inconsiderable, varying from 2/8d to 3/6d for a four-line minimum in *The Chronicle*, *Standard*, and *Globe*, and a hefty two shillings per line in *The Times*. The six-line notice which led to the solution of *The Adventure of the Naval Treaty* had cost me nearly two weeks' Army pension which I had failed to recover from Holmes. I resigned myself to another attack on my insubstantial pocket. With our lives at stake there was nothing to do but pursue the subterfuge. I took out my note-book.

'I'm ready, Holmes,' I said. 'Would you like to give me the wording?'

'Commence with the heading *Substantial Remuneration, not less than 150 Guineas*, followed by, *Wanted. Guide well acquainted with Ceylon, in particular Adam's Peak. Knowledge of Tamil and Arwi useful. All expenses. Able to leave immediately for up to three months. Apply by letter to Mr. Sherlock Holmes of 221B, Baker Street, London.*

'That should do it,' he ended. 'I suggest you send it to all the newspapers Moran might conceivably read, including the morning editions.' Holmes pointed to *Lloyds List*.

'I've checked the movement of ships. The newest and largest Jubilees of the Peninsular and Oriental sail weekly from the London Docks to Aden and points east. The next liner to sail is the *Victoria*. We shall let it be known we intend go by train to France and board her at Marseilles, thereby avoiding the Bay of Biscay at this time of the year. Our guide must go aboard in London. He'll be halfway to India before he can check out the entire passenger list – every decrepit Italian priest, every down-on-his-luck goatee beard and a swagger. To boot, Moran will lose himself a pocketful of money for the return fare.'

'What of Adam's Peak?' I asked.

'On the summit of the mountain is a single footprint revered by all three Eastern religions. To the Buddhist it is where the

Gautama momentarily rested his foot on his flight to Heaven. For the Moslem it is where Adam, having been expelled from the Garden of Eden, stood on one leg for a thousand years before being reunited with Eve on Mount Ararat.'

'And to the Hindu?'

'It's the Sacred Footprint of Siva, the god of destruction and regeneration.'

I frowned. 'Why would Moran find Adam's Peak of interest? He's not known to be a connoisseur of Eastern religions.'

'The peak's above 7000 feet,' Holmes continued. 'It can only be reached from the village of Maskeliya by a journey of some eight miles on foot over open mountainside. Moran will envisage many a nook and cranny among the vegetation and rocks to exercise his trigger finger. Given the occasional elephant trampling through the tea-plantations, he is perfectly entitled to carry a bespoke double rifle.'

I replaced my notebook in a pocket.

'Oh, and Watson, given the high possibility that the deceased Moriarty's tentacles have spread into Cox's Bank, on your way back please call in at the bank for some rupees. Then, as a treat, I suggest we invite Mrs. Hudson to prepare us a dozen oysters and a couple of brace of cold woodcock, followed by a bottle of that choice little Ferreira Garrafeira Vintage Port 1863 delivered to us at the instance of your friend, the Prince Regnant of Bulgaria.'

I had reached the door when my comrade called out to me in an unusually serious tone.

'If anything happens to me because of our trip, don't have me cremated before you have removed the £1000 banknote stitched into the lining of these trousers. That should be enough to get you home and a little more besides.'

***

I decided to purchase two one-thousand rupee banknotes and a suitable assembly of ten-rupee notes with as much ostentation as possible and our Swiss francs with the least. My walk took me through the Inns of Court. I halted for a moment outside the Henry Fielding Hotel, my first lodgings on returning from Afghanistan. The hotel rates (albeit including illuminating gas) were uncomfortably high for my wound-pension. Recollections flooded back. Though I missed the camaraderie of the regimental mess, I was glad enough to exchange the cobra of the Afghan hills for our common adder, although bitter that Afghanistan had taken away youth, strength and energy and left me with a damaged *tendo Achillis*. Set against this, my time on the North West Frontier had left me with a vast accumulated knowledge of the science of medicine.

The bank manager handed me the rupees. Would he also, I asked casually, provide me with a supply of Swiss currency – explaining that the Swiss francs were for a trip following our return from Ceylon.

'Dr. Watson,' he replied expansively, 'English sovereigns and bank-notes are gladly received everywhere. Why should you and Mr. Sherlock Holmes concern yourself with the Swiss franc?'

The bank manager peered through his spectacles at a list on his desk.

'Though as a convenience, you might hold a few guineas' worth of small Swiss notes. An English sovereign will get you 25 francs. I am told that a comfortable hotel will charge you four or five francs for bedroom, light and attendance, and perhaps a further twelve francs for all meals, plus small tips for the boots and porter.'

The sound of people engaged in fierce argument burst in on us. Two men locked in each other's clasp fell through the door, the one an elderly cleric, the other a member of the bank's staff trying to prevent his entry. High-pitched tones emanated from the priest as he pushed himself into the room past the employee. Under a wrap-rascal he wore baggy trousers and white tie, topped by a broad black hat, the exact dress of the Nonconformist clergyman I described in *A Scandal In Bohemia*. He demanded to speak to the bank manager come what may, insisting he needed to open a safe deposit box on the instant, 'poor as a church mouse as those of my calling may be'.

With a triumphant flourish at having gained entry, the clergyman dropped a heavy pouch on the manager's desk. It was the very pouch of gold coins given to us by the Prince Regnant of Bulgaria five years before. The purse split with the force of the fall, scattering the glittering coins across the desk and into every corner of the room.

At the sight of the gold coins the bank manager rushed around the desk and waved the staff member away.

'I am sure Dr. Watson will not mind if we are joined by a clergyman,' he expostulated. 'I myself am a son of the manse, with a strict Presbyterian upbringing.'

'Not at all,' I responded amiably. 'The clergyman is most welcome.'

My Heavens, I thought. Holmes has gone a step too far. He will be found out within a matter of minutes. I turned to the bank manager.

'You say you are a son of the manse?' I enquired.

'I am,' he replied. 'Every day my aged father proclaims the sovereignty of God, the authority of the Scriptures, and the necessity of grace through faith in Christ.'

'Then I am sure our clergyman friend here would enjoy sharing his knowledge of the Sacred Book. A short test, perhaps?'

Embarrassed, the bank manager began to protest. Holmes cut back in.

'Come now, Sir,' he told the bank manager, gesturing towards me, 'as our young friend here demands, you must question me. Test the simple preacher seated before you on his knowledge of the Scriptures.'

The bank manager agreed, immeasurably pleased. 'The Epistle of Paul to the Church at Philippi,' he began,' the book of the Gospel where…'

'*Acts*, Sir,' Holmes broke in, chortling. 'You shall have to do better than that.'

'Which book? Ninth, I believe?' asked the son of the manse.

'Eleventh,' Holmes returned.

'But you agree it was written on St. Paul's first missionary journey?'

'Second,' Holmes parried.

'Date?'

'49-51 AD,' Holmes ended, triumphantly.

'I too have a question,' I broke in.

It was a question my Tractarian mother had once posed on my return from Sunday School.

'Where in the Bible does it refer to 'Five Golden Emerods' and 'five golden mice'? Kings or Chronicles – or Ruth?' I asked.

'Good, Watson,' Holmes whispered, 'but not good enough!' followed aloud by 'Samuel, my dear fellow. 1 Samuel 6:4 if I am not mistaken.'

Heavens, Holmes, I thought admiringly. The stage may have lost a great actor when you took up crime, but the Church lost a doughty scholar. I realised he took his own counsel seriously. To adopt a disguise was not simply a matter of clothing, posture, expression or make-up. Indispensable skills for a detective masquerading as Holmes did as a plumber or groom meant mingling with the working classes or even the destitute in London's slums, to absorb all their accents and mannerisms.

With the rupees and Swiss bank-notes tucked securely under my coat, I left the clergyman and bank manager still discussing matters Biblical, and resolved to purchase a copy of William Clark Russell's latest nautical novel *The Mystery of the Ocean Star* for the journey to the Swiss Alps.

At Marshall & Snelgrove's I ordered a suit of pongee silk, white drill, and a Swiss Army officer's knife Modell 1890. From there I strolled in open view. Whenever I could be lost to sight in the crowded streets I slowed my pace to allow an observer to regain my trail. At Salmon & Gluckstein of Oxford Street – 'Largest and Cheapest Tobacconists in the World' – I purchased a half-dozen tins of J&H Wilson No. 1 Top Mill snuff and a box of Churchwarden clay pipes, proclaiming loudly that the latter were presents for the natives. I announced extravagantly how appreciative Holmes and I would be if the Tobacconist supplied us with several boxes of Trichinopoly cigars manufactured from tobacco grown near the town of Dindigul ('a favourite of yellow-robed Buddhist monks,' I explained to the small audience around me).

My next stop was Foyle's bookshop at Cecil Court for *The Mystery of the Ocean Star*. From there I strolled openly to Watson & Sons in Holborn where I usually purchased my microscope slides. The same photographic suppliers stocked the wide-angle photographic lenses suited to Alpine and no doubt Adam's Peak vistas. My final call was on B. J. Edwards for Iso plates.

On my return, I found Holmes in our living-room, bent over a large survey map brought across Hyde Park from the hallowed vaults of the Royal Geographical Society. A life preserver, a new box of Manstopper bullets 'for police, civilian and Colonial use', and a tin of Rangoon Oil sat by the map. A brand-new Webley Metropolitan Police revolver with a lanyard-ring lay beside him. The two-and-a-half inch barrel allowed the weapon to be secreted in the trouser waistband or pocket of an Inverness cloak. I looked dubiously at the hand-gun. Holmes was more than my equal with a rifle but his principal experience with a handgun had been desultory practice many years earlier on a range among sand-dunes near Calais. I glanced over Holmes's shoulder at the map.

'Holmes,' I exclaimed, 'do I deduce that you are studying our choice of tracks to the Reichenbach Falls?'

He put the magnifying glass down. 'Really, Watson, you excel yourself. Palpably your walk has cleared the brain.'

He folded the map and applied a lightly oiled ramrod to the barrel of the revolver. The oiling complete, he dry-fired the weapon three times and put it back on the table.

'If our deceit fails and Moran catches up with us on those mountainous slopes, we shall have need of all the fire-power we can muster. Not a word must reach Moran's ears as to our real enterprise or we are doomed,' he warned.

'I can assure you, Holmes, I have extracted the firmest of promises from my publisher,' I returned. 'Not a syllable will escape his lips, not to the English newspapers, not even to his wife and children.'

'I have no worries in a town as busy as Berne,' Holmes said, 'but don't make a reservation for us at our former hotel at the Falls. Old Steiler will surely forgive us. We must take a chance on rooms. We'll arrive after dark at the Hotel Sauvage, unannounced and using our new sobriquets.'

**

The following morning I strolled into our sitting room to find Holmes once more poring over the silk-panelled map with a magnifying lens. He looked up.

'Do you still wish to become the asthmatic captain of the *Roi des Belges* steaming up the Congo River?' he queried.

'No, Holmes. On our past adventures you have limited me to a moustache here, a pair of rubbish-collector's boots there, or for our adventure at Scotney Castle, a country-cut coat and low-crowned hat. This time I fancy passing myself off as an Ambassador,' I responded.

41

'While you have a good line in pomposity, Watson,' Holmes replied, grinning, 'what if you get carried away and describe the wounds caused by the Long Tom cannon used to pound the Afghan tribesmen? Colonel Moran would detect your Army station in an instant.'

He thought for a moment and snapped his fingers.

'I have it! We shall take on the appearance which accords most closely to our purpose in being at the Falls. Photographers! Taking photographs of waterfalls for the London Hydraulic Power Company postal cards. You may abandon the Ascot-knotted cravat and pin and your rigid conventional dress with its smell of camphor. Embrace the high collar and black frock-coat embellished by yellow gloves, white waistcoat, patent leather shoes and light-coloured gaiters.'

He paused. 'Unless of course, for a reason I would find unfathomable, you prefer to be a missionary of the Colonial and Continental Church Society, or a decayed professor studying archaeology?'

'If I am to play the role of photographer, what about you?'

'Your assistant, what else? I must not steal your thunder. I'll need nothing more than a Norfolk suit with a spare pair of breeches. I shall name myself George Archibald Hewitt.'

'And I?' I asked, amused.

'How about Samuel Learson?' came the reply. 'We'll be Hewitt and Learson, Photographers. I doubt if hotel-keepers or even the police in the Bernese Oberland bother to learn the names of England's foremost forger or safe-breaker. To complete our masquerade we'll order a pair of bicycles and pedal them with abandon.'

Mrs. Hudson's brother-in-law sent over an advertisement claiming Mohair Sicilian was far and away the best variety of cloth for cycling purposes. 'The coarse weave renders it not only more appropriate for the wheel, but causes it to retain its style and lustre under the most severe strain which the ardent cyclist can put upon it.'

For the next few days my breakfasts were accompanied by a copy of *Cycling Magazine* Vol. X1V. The cover story informed me that the magnificent Purple Emperor butterfly abounds in Hyde and Battersea parks, and had even been observed in stately flight in the neighbourhood of Richmond. A less peaceable use of the bicycle came with a full-page advertisement titled 'The Bicycle in War'. 'Can a bicycle be satisfactorily used in real warfare?' it asked. The noted war correspondent, Mr. Wilfred Pollock said it could. He went through the Graeco-Turkish campaign on a Raleigh with Dunlop tyres, despite the rough roads of Thessaly. 'This machine was ridden over a barley field and came out all right' and 'Dispensing entirely with horses and using the bicycle alone he saw every fight except the first and was able to beat all other war correspondents in the dispatch of news.'

I mooted the idea of a tandem. Holmes rejected it out of hand.

'We must do nothing that would encourage attention, Watson. In the entire history of mankind it is impossible to think of a more ludicrous sight than you and me attacking an Alpine slope on a tandem.'

Knowing Holmes's notorious reluctance to dress appropriately on public occasions, I entered his dressing-room to check his wardrobe for the ceremony in Berne. The only coat in evidence was his favourite loose Ulster, the sole headgear a rural outdoorsman's rabbit-skin cap with hanging lappets. I told Holmes the occasion called for a swallow tail coat, white waistcoat and white bow tie. He would be representing not just himself but England. Open warfare was on the point of breaking out.

Two hours later he returned bearing a borrowed deerstalker and an overcoat with a velvet collar worthy of a senior partner in a large private banking concern. The dispute continued. Holmes offered a compromise. He would pack a new frock coat or a black lounge jacket. If it was good enough for Simpsons...

In the end we compromised. Holmes gave in to a double-breasted frock coat from Scholte's with its characteristic unpadded shoulders, plus a waistcoat and Ascot tie.

***

Our advertisement seeking a guide for Adam's Peak received two replies. We discarded the clearly genuine response. 'Dear Mr. Ranawana, unfortunately your reply arrived too late,' I wrote. The other applicant had Moran's footprints all over it. It said he was 'English born' and stressed his suitability 'from many years in the sub-Continent and a facility with languages'. If we found his qualifications satisfactory, we should reply to a given postal box with our final instructions. Our response instructed him to purchase a second-class ticket for the *Victoria*. He was to board her in London. He could give his forwarding address as the Grand Oriental Hotel, Colombo. On arrival in Ceylon he would be given time to purchase a few necessities at Whiteaway, Laidlaw & Co. We assured him that he would be compensated on arrival. I had no intention of doing so if it proved to be Moran.

From that point on we presumed we were under the constant gaze of Moran. We engaged the half-dozen little Street Arabs known to us as the Baker Street Irregulars. A few bags of maroon-coloured Norfolk Biffins purchased from a cart and a shilling per day per ragamuffin guaranteed they were the finest flock of look-outs London could supply. I saved up my officer's half-pay pension for an eve-of-departure dinner at the restaurant run by Josef Sheekey, unrivalled in London for fish and seafood dishes. An elegantly dressed doorman of unimposing politeness and gentility, complete with top hat, greeted us outside the wine-red shop front. We were led to rich red leather banquettes. The warm, dark wood panelling was dotted with paintings of Hastings trawlers by the artist Barbara Bodichon. I ordered Colchester oysters and Cornish cock-crab.

Chapter IV

We Return to Switzerland

After a fine night's sleep, I awoke with inexpressible happiness. I would be at my comrade's side once more as we ventured abroad. A driver came to the door at eight o'clock. We stepped into the vehicle with the air of men without a care in the world, accompanied by the camera and tripod and a *vasculum* for collecting specimens of exotic plants. I had decided against a hansom hailed from the street in favour of a chauffeured, 16-horsepower Maxwell touring car with bevel-gear drive. The Maxwell could outpace any horse-drawn transport determined to follow us. A barouche hired from Shipley's Yard followed behind, loaded to the gunnels with trunks filled only with old newspapers, ostentatiously covered with shipping labels for points East. The bogus impedimenta would be lodged overnight at No. 10 Downing Street care of Mycroft and quietly retrieved by our loyal Mrs. Hudson. We would catch the next boat train to Paris, and to all appearances travel on to Marseilles to pick up the great ocean liner.

We boarded the train at Victoria Station, our first trip together for some years. As we rattled through the Sussex countryside I stared across at Holmes. Inheritance had bequeathed him considerable height, the prominent, penetrating grey eyes and square chin. It was at university and its slow aftermath that the elements came together to form the great Consulting Detective, like an actor assembling a character from costume and prop to the final full performance. The pipe, the ear-flapped hat, the ever-present rudeness and arrogance, the curious sense of humour. The next day we arrived in Berne. The University had arranged comfortable accommodation for us at the Hotel Sternen Muri. We found ourselves with a day to reorient ourselves comfortably. I felt secure in the belief that, thanks to our precautions, we had not been followed to Switzerland.

It was now the day of the ceremony. An open carriage took us to the University, the plumed horses regal enough to take King Edward himself from Buckingham Palace to the State opening of Parliament. Pedestrians and cyclists stopped to watch as we swept by. We arrived at our destination, a large new building on the Grosse Schanze. A man in late middle age met us. Keen eyes sparkled brightly from behind large horn glasses. He bowed ceremoniously in our direction.

'Gentlemen, I am Professor Eli Sobel,' he explained in good but heavily-accented English. 'Head of the Department of Physics.'

He led us up the imposing stairway and along a broad, high-ceilinged corridor to an ante-chamber set up as a gentleman's cloakroom. A collection of costly silk toppers perched on shelves to the left. Pegs to the right held modest Quakers and a fedora to which I added Holmes's felt hat and my billycock. We continued on to a side-entrance to await the arrival of the Rector and dignitaries. Vases crammed with flowers lined the walls like wall-paintings from a Roman villa. Excited groups of people flocked into an auditorium where the ceremony would take place. Dowager lorgnettes, ruffles, fluted collars, lace flounces and *bris*-fans bristled with social warfare.

I was led to a seat in the front row. The procession entered to a fanfare of trumpets, headed by the Usher with a gold-tipped mace. He was followed by the Rector and Holmes, side by side with Professor Sobel. Behind them straggled dark-suited Faculty members. Holmes settled himself into the graduand's red-plush and gold-embellished chair. The Rector strode to the podium to a polite and expectant hush. He spoke first in German, then followed it with the French translation.

'Minister, Your Honour the Mayor, Monsieur Chapuiset of the *Journal de Genève*, Faculty members, Distinguished Friends, citizenry of Berne, our graduand Mr. Sherlock Holmes and not least our graduand's own thane, Dr. John Hamish Watson, the very equal of Suetonius.'

At my side the polyglot student assigned to be my interpreter whispered the English translation. I flushed.

Resplendent in scarlet robes, the tall, sandy-moustached Orator surveyed the audience with scrutinising eyes through rimless pince-nez. He then moved to the front of the stage. Fluent in Latin and Ancient Greek, he began to speak.

'The honour we confer to-day is a rare one. An *Honoris Causa* was last bestowed on the artist Albert Samuel Anke, known as the 'national painter of Switzerland' for his depictions of village life. Our recipient to-day would also merit it for art, the art of deduction. He is the epitome of deductive brilliance not only in his native England, but in Norway, Bulgaria, and America and many other lands, including our own dear Switzerland. He is a more commanding figure in the world than most warriors and statesmen. Like the greatest of them, Mr. Sherlock Holmes is a *redresseur de destins*. Who here does not recall the account in *Le Journal de Genève* in May 1891 of the near-mythic struggle at our Reichenbach Falls – the clash of Titans – between the most dangerous criminal of the Age and the foremost champion of the Law? The gargantuan tussle ended with the death of Professor Moriarty of mathematical celebrity, and the presumed death of to-day's guest himself.'

'But it is not for Mr. Holmes's pre-eminence in crime detection that we honour him to-day. He is being awarded a Doctorate *honoris causa* for his pioneering work in Physical Chemistry, specifically the scientific study of organic substances at the molecular scale, primarily with gases.'

The Orator turned to address Holmes directly.

'Mr. Sherlock Holmes, you are receiving this honour to-day because you have used your knowledge of chemical poisons for the benefit of Mankind. This knowledge enabled you to identify murderers in the cases of *The Greek Interpreter* and *The Retired Colourman*; and to deter a suicide in *The Veiled Lodger*. Your pioneering test for the presence of blood was a significant advance in forensic methods. You are indeed master of the Principle of Sufficient Reason, the basis of all science. How aptly Aristotle put it, πᾶσα ἐπιστήμη διανοητική, ἢ καί μετέχουσά τι διανοίας, περί αἰτίας...'

The Orator paused. His eye swept across the audience.

'Ah,' he continued. 'For those of you not conversant with Ancient Greek, the Roman would say, '*Omnis intellectualis scientia, sive aliquo modo intellectu, participans, circa causas et principia est*'.'

The display of erudition triggered enthusiastic applause. Professor Sobel beckoned Holmes to stand and approach the Rector to be solemnly dressed in doctoral robes and hat. Further enthusiastic applause arose when my comrade, in his fine regalia, bowed to the audience. The ceremony ended, the procession reformed and left the stage.

At the end of a convivial reception, Holmes and I shook hands with the Rector and Orator and retraced our steps with Professor Sobel to the cloakroom. *En route* the Professor remarked conversationally, 'It might interest you to know, Mr. Holmes, that in the month following your encounter with Professor Moriarty at the Reichenbach Falls, the Rector was due to confer upon him precisely the same honour you received today, an Honorary Doctorate for his remarkable *Dynamics of an Asteroid*. If it hadn't been for his sudden demise it would have been merely a matter of time before we offered him a Chair.'

We emerged by a side-entrance into the outside world. The Professor hesitated. For a moment it seemed he was about to say something further. If so, he decided against it. With a courteous nod he left us at our resplendent open coach and pair. Ceremony was behind us. Ahead lay Meiringen, the Reichenbach Falls, and the photograph.

***

On the journey from Berne into the Alps, Moran crept back into my thoughts. Nearly three weeks had passed since the *Victoria* was due to set sail for the Mediterranean Sea and beyond. I wondered whether our subterfuge had thrown him off our tracks. Reassurance was in the offing. A telegraph awaited us at the Hotel Sauvage under our assumed names. Holmes passed the envelope to me. I opened it and read aloud:

'Gulf of Aden. From the Master of the *Victoria* to Messrs. Hewitt and Learson. Private. We coaled last night in Aden. Next stop Bombay. Man answering your description aboard. Singled himself out by displaying exceptional prowess in the clay-pigeon shooting competition through the Suez Canal.'

'Excellent! Well done, Holmes!' I exclaimed. 'I shall look forward to Moran sending us a half-anna pictorial postcard from British India. By the time he discovers the large operatic lady at the next table is neither you nor me, he will have the entire return journey to take his revenge on clay pigeons. If we manage to keep our presence here secret until we have visited the Falls and completed our mission, we can return safely to England.'

Holmes waggled a finger. 'Don't cry herrings till they are in the net, Watson. Nevertheless,' he added, 'for the moment it seems Moran is *hors de combat.*'

The bicycles we had ordered from Paris arrived, two *Le Globe Modèle-Extra-Luxe* with Dunlop tyres, at a road-ready weight of 12 kilogrammes, 320 French francs apiece. They were the most beautiful machines imaginable.

Holmes eyed them. 'How do they work, Watson?' he asked.

Surprised, I responded, 'You get on them and pedal.'

'That I know,' came the long-suffering reply. 'I mean, what law of physics keeps the contraptions upright while you pedal?'

'The gyroscopic force of the front wheel, do you think?' I hazarded.

'No doubt, but if we take into account the distribution of weight, the handlebar turn and the angles of the headset and the forks, the gyroscopic effect would not be enough.'

'Then I am sure I don't know, Holmes,' I replied. 'Experience tells me that while we pedal, these machines will stay upright. When we stop, they won't.'

'Like the dark side of the moon and the three-body problem,' I added, philosophically, 'some things may remain a mystery for a very long time.'

In the late afternoon we assembled in the hotel smoking-room. Cigars were in full blow, sending up blue spirals with nothing in the still air to trouble them. Holmes and I stared through the window in the direction of the Reichenbach River. The famous Falls were set too deep in the mountainside for the roar of tumbling waters to reach our ears. Before dining I left Holmes and stepped outside. All the familiar landmarks met my eyes. I determined I would reconnoitre the immediate area of the Falls in the morning for the ideal spot for the photograph. This would best be undertaken without Holmes tugging impatiently at my elbow.

On the morrow the hotel delivered a supply of English newspapers to our room. I provided my comrade with an ounce of shag from our stock of Bradley's. He sat smoking his pipe, framed by an unmatched view of the icy peaks rearing above us. He looked up and waved a hand around him.

'Watson, how small we feel in the presence of such elemental forces! How clear it becomes that we are merely three buckets of water and a tray full of chemicals.'

I reflected on how it took a vast mountain range to make Holmes break into a statement of such rare modesty. I left him on the terrace reading contentedly through the pile of newspapers. To retain our anonymity, I decided against the electric funicular in favour of a two-horse drag, carrying a tin vasculum in the fine tradition of botanists scouring the world's wildernesses. Despite the reassuring information from the Master of the *Victoria*, I paid the fare well short of my destination and waited until the cabbie set back before continuing my journey on foot.

Alone with my thoughts and unburdened by cumbersome photographic equipment, I wended my way along the same thin path I had taken fourteen years ago. In the early summer light the Alps were as beautiful as I remembered them. The meadows and high rocky ground blazed with spring flowers – cowslips, Lady's Mantle, vivid blue spring gentian and Edelweiss. Higher up in rocky areas lurked the tall Common Monkshood, pointed out by Holmes on our earlier climb. Despite its beautiful blue blossoms it was one of the most deadly plants of European and Himalayan flora. In ancient times, people coated spears and arrowheads with its poison, strong enough to kill wolves.

The gorge began to narrow, leaving a sliver of sky half way between blue and green. The torrent burst into view. There, in my imagination, was Holmes's Alpine-stock still leaning against the rock, there the ledge on which Holmes had placed his farewell note fluttering beneath his precious silver cigarette case. I could recall the words almost by heart.

My dear Watson,

I write these few lines through the courtesy of Mr. Moriarty, who awaits my convenience for the final discussion of those questions which lie between us. He has been giving me a sketch of the methods by which he avoided the English police and kept himself informed of our movements. They certainly confirm the very high opinion which I had formed of his abilities. I am pleased to think that I shall be able to free society from any further effects of his presence, though I fear that it is at a cost which will give pain to my friends, and especially, my dear Watson, to you. I have already explained to you, however, that my career had in any case reached its crisis, and that no possible conclusion to it could be more congenial to me than this.

Tell Inspector Patterson that the papers which he needs to convict the gang are in pigeonhole M, done up in a blue envelope and inscribed 'Moriarty'. I made every disposition of my property before leaving England, and handed it to my brother Mycroft...

Believe me to be, my dear fellow,

Very sincerely yours,

Sherlock Holmes

The letter had ended with greetings to my now-deceased wife, Mary.

I reached the site I had in mind for the photograph, a wide rock platform. It was not the exact spot where the death struggle took place, but the camera angle would work better to show the terrifying force of the plunging waters. A short distance away stood the ruins of a building where I could hide the photographic apparatus, tucked away from the spray, until Holmes arrived to take up his position. Perhaps it was the result of my exertions or the effect of the rushing waters on my brain, but in my imagination I could picture crouching figures behind every jutting bush and rock.

I retraced my footsteps down to our hotel and greeted my comrade with a 'How are you, Holmes?'

The unusual dilation of his pupils caught my attention. He thrust a newspaper at me.

'Watson, I deduce from your question they do not sell the English edition of the *Journal de Genève* at the Reichenbach Falls.'

Concerned by his tone, I grabbed the newspaper and sped quickly through the first article.

'ICEMAN EXPOSED BY MELTING GLACIER – PRESERVED NATURAL MUMMY OF MAN WHO LIVED ABOUT 3,200 YEARS AGO.'

The article continued,

Ice-melt at the Rosenlaui Glacier has revealed the mummified corpse of an iceman some 1.65 metres tall. Initial examination by the University of Berne pathology department estimates he weighed about 50 kilogrammes at death and was about 45 years of age. Intestinal contents show two meals, one of chamois meat, the other of red deer and herb bread. He was clad in a cloak of woven grass and a coat, a belt, a pair of leggings, a loincloth and shoes, all made of leather of different skins. Other items found with the Iceman were a copper axe with a yew handle, a flint-bladed knife with an ash handle and a quiver of 14 arrows with viburnum and dogwood shafts.

I looked up at Holmes. 'This is a wonderful discovery, Holmes, do you suspect foul play – ?'

'Watson!' Holmes exploded, 'not that wretched iceman and his copper axe – the piece below!'

The headline blared 'WORLD'S MOST FAMOUS CRIMINAL AGENT RETURNS TO MEIRINGEN'.

For the first time since the epic struggle on the 4th of May 1891 (as reported in this newspaper), during which he ended the life of the arch-criminal Professor Moriarty, Mr. Sherlock Holmes has returned to Meiringen, accompanied by his amanuensis, Dr. John Watson. The notable pair arrived in Switzerland earlier this week at the invitation of the Rector of Berne University. The University conferred an Honorary Doctorate on Mr. Holmes for outstanding services to the Natural Sciences. The *Journal* understands that Dr. Watson has been commissioned by the mass circulation *Strand Magazine* to take a photograph of the eminent Consulting Detective at the very ledge overlooking the Reichenbach Falls where the epic struggle took place. All Europe remembers the events of that day. By his actions Sherlock Holmes rid the world of the Number One enemy of propriety and justice and made it a safer place for all.

My heart thumped.

Sir George Newnes had kept strictly to his word not to reveal our movements to the London newspapers, but - no doubt in the hope of increasing the Strand's circulation among English-speaking residents on the Continent – he had informed the *Journal de Genève* without realising the Reuter Agency or the Central Press Syndicate would most certainly pick up the report for distribution to news-sheets worldwide.

'Holmes,' I spluttered, 'perhaps Moran will fail to hear about our presence here. After all, he is far away in the midst of the Indian Ocean.'

'Perhaps,' came the uncertain reply.

During the first few nights at altitude I sleep fitfully. That night I was even more restless than usual. At last I fell into a slumber. A light tap at the door made me sit up abruptly.

'Very sorry to wake you,' came Holmes's voice. 'Turn just the one table-lamp on, there's a good fellow. News has arrived from London. When you are dressed, meet me on the terrace where we can be alone.'

I joined Holmes in the dim pre-dawn light.

Still groggy, I protested, 'Holmes, would it be too much to ask why you have summoned me at – ', I consulted my pocket watch, 'Good Lord! It's half-past four in the morning!'

'Clearly our use of substitute names failed to work, Watson.'

He held up two telegrams. 'These were brought straight to me.'

One was addressed to 'Mr. Sherlock Holmes or Dr. John Watson'. It read:

Mr. Holmes,
Told no one of your whereabouts. London newspapers revealed your presence. Ten reporters came to door in middle of night. Obliged to quit house by back window into yard. If necessary can reach me at sisters.
Regards, M. Hudson.

'Now read this second telegram,' Holmes ordered. It was from the *Victoria*. Its terse wording read:

From the Captain. Arabia Sea. Urgent.
Attention Messrs. Hewitt & Learson.
English newspaper reports telegraphed to ship contain details of Honour conferred on Sherlock Holmes by University of Berne and return to Meiringen. Passenger in earlier communication composed telegram to London in following code. Two words not encoded Reichenbach Falls.

The message was followed by a page covered by a series of three numbers separated by full stops.

It was clear that Colonel Moran had issued an order from the Arabian Sea to his footpads at the murderous Lower Rung Club. I felt dizzy with shock. We would need to abandon all thought of continuing with our photographic enterprise.

'Holmes,' I began, 'we must at once – '

He interrupted me. 'Watson, this code is based on *Blackstone's Commentaries on the Laws of England*. I myself have used it on several occasions. Each word is described by three numbers, giving page, line and position of the word in that line.'

Holmes's bony finger jabbed at the middle of the page. 'If I recall correctly, this set, namely 22.9.14, stands for "Arrival".' His finger drifted back along the lines of numerals.

'And 102.8.26,' he continued.

'Stands for?'

'"Essential",' came the reply. 'As to the rest, without Blackstone's I have reached my limit. I lodge my copy of Blackstone's with Mycroft. He keeps it at No. 10 Downing Street where it looks perfectly in place. We must telegraph the coded message to my brother immediately, with instructions to wake him from his slumber. I suggest we get a couple of hours' more sleep. The moment I receive Mycroft's reply I shall share it with you.'

***

Dawn was breaking when we reassembled on the terrace. The response from Mycroft arrived with a pot of coffee. My comrade pondered for a few seconds before flicking the page across the broad table.

'Mycroft has deciphered Moran's telegram.'

The decoded message was shorter than I had anticipated from the jumble of numbers. It read:

> Aboard the Victoria. Essential you do not proceed to Reichenbach Falls. Cover quarry's' arrival at likely Channel ports, not least Continental boat trains between Newhaven and London. SM.

'You will note even our greatest living adversary forgets himself in his excitement,' Holmes remarked with a slight smile. 'To his minions, Sebastian Moran has signed himself with his true initials, yet aboard the *Victoria* he will be known by the quite different *nomme de guerre* he supplied to us.'

A surge of relief burst through me.

'Holmes,' I exclaimed, 'it seems we are safe! Moran says explicitly 'do not proceed to the Reichenbach Falls'. We shall be able to take the photograph after all.'

Holmes's fingers unwrapped themselves from a long cherry-wood pipe. In a serious tone he resumed.

'I must inform you, my dear Watson, that your conclusions are erroneous. We are in the utmost danger and must quit this hotel with all due speed.'

I stared in bewilderment at my companion.

Holmes continued, 'It tells us that if the Channel is calm, the first of Moran's assassins should arrive here in a matter of hours. My brother is a cryptographer of great merit and intuition. Moran's telegram has made him suspicious in the extreme. The message ends, 534 C2 13 127 – followed by 36 31 4 17 21 etc. Those numerals and the letter C were added by Mycroft. As children he and I communicated using a code based on the old Whitaker's Almanac our father revered. We used that particular warning frequently enough to fix it firmly in my memory. It means danger may come very soon.'

I responded, 'Nevertheless, in his telegram Moran orders his band of assassins to waylay us at the Channel, not here in the middle of Switzerland.'

Holmes looked again at the telegram.

'Colonel Moran moves up in my estimation,' he said. 'Something of Moriarty has rubbed off on him. It was genius on Moran's part. Leaving the words Reichenbach Falls uncoded means he has worked out that the *Victoria*'s Captain is in communication with us. Moran knew I would come quickly to the realisation he was using *Blackstone*'s, ergo he wanted us to break his code. He must have read my monograph on codes where I recommend *Blackstone's*. If Colonel Moran anticipated that we would break the code, it can mean only one thing: he has a long-standing arrangement with the recipients that they will do precisely the opposite. 'Wait for us at the Channel ports'? No – it means they are not to wait for us at the Channel ports. 'Do not proceed to the Reichenbach Falls' – *do* proceed. Hardly shall we have pedalled furiously from here than they will be taking up their hiding-places on the slopes above us.'

'If you are correct in your deduction, Holmes, then we must slip away at once,' I said. 'One shot from a rifle as powerful as those Moran would provide for his acolytes would shatter our skulls into splinters.'

'We must adjust our plans in light of this new information,' Holmes responded. 'I shall be infinitely obliged if you will find a hotel servant and order him to bring us a further pot of coffee while I change to a new pipe. If we are to relinquish limb or life in carrying out your commission, this may be the last quiet talk that we shall ever have.'

I got to my feet. 'If your deduction is correct, Holmes,' I responded, 'rather than a pot of coffee and a fireside chat we must abandon the photograph and make our way back to England without a moment's delay.'

My companion looked at me calmly. 'Tell me, Watson, where had you thought to secure the photograph for the *Strand*?'

'The exact spot where you tossed Moriarty to his death – where else?' I replied.

'At the very same cliff edge?' Holmes pursued.

'Preferably, yes,' I replied.

'And how long will the photograph take?'

'At least the quarter hour. My instructions are to get your face in sharp detail, with a determined look on it, the torrent in soft focus at your back,' I explained. 'But surely that is entirely academic. We – .'

'So we would be *en plein air* and in good light long enough for the worst marksmen in the world to loose at least a hundred shots at us,' Holmes interrupted.

'Let me ask you a question,' he continued. 'There are seventy-two waterfalls in the Bernese Oberland. Of your countless readers, how many will have visited each of them in person?'

I attempted a smile. 'A handful at most. I've heard the expression that when you have seen one Alp you have seen them all. I believe much the same applies to Alpine falls.'

I ordered the pot of coffee and instructed the waiter to take the pot together with the hotel bill to the terrace. I sped to my room to pack my few belongings. When I rejoined Holmes on the otherwise empty terrace he was staring at the guide-book. All seemed tranquil. The sun was by now high over a fine mountain peak. Our bicycles awaited us. At my arrival he looked up and swept a hand across the landscape.

'Tell me,' he asked, 'what do you make of such a view! Doesn't it bring out the poetry in a man's soul. You know, Watson, every time you and I confront the Grim Reaper's rapscallions, I am forced to wonder about the Life Hereafter.'

Holmes continued, 'At the very least, after we are gone, I believe a vaporous emanation of our lives will linger on until everyone who knew us has also departed.'

'Holmes, without question I accept Hamlet's argument there may well be more things in Heaven and Earth, but could we get on, please?'

'Certainly, Watson, but first I have a further question. Are you prepared to play just the smallest of deceits on your publisher?'

I replied cautiously, 'What are you suggesting?'

Holmes reached into a pocket and withdrew his *Baedeker* guide book. He waved the stocky volume at me and read out loud:

'"The narrow gorge, with the copious brook fed by the glaciers, is rendered accessible by steps and rough paths. The sun forms beautiful rainbows in the spray which bedews trees and meadows far and wide".'

'Holmes, I am fully apprised of such descriptions of the Reichenbach Falls,' I retorted. 'You may recall I was with you only minutes before you plunged Moriarty to his death.'

Holmes's eyes sparkled. He sent up a great blue triumphant cloud from the briar pipe and slid the guide book across the table.

'Turn to Page 192.'

I did as ordered. Astonished, I exclaimed, 'The passage you read refers to the Falls on the Trümmelbach, yet it could hardly be bettered as a description of the Reichenbach.'

'Precisely. For the fifteen minutes or so required for your photograph, given an exact angle, the Trümmelbach Falls will become the Reichenbach Falls. Hats and boots, Watson! Our *hegira* commences.'

Holmes flicked the hotel bill across to me.

'Deal with this, there's a good fellow. Tell them the telegrams require us to return at once to Interlaken. Ask about trains. Mention in passing that we shall be travelling on to Tuscany by the quickest route. Our real destination lies in the opposite direction.'

***

We set off for our new destination, driving hard on the bicycle pedals until my lungs panted in the thin air. The bulky camera and tripod were due to follow us to the Stechtelberg by dog-cart. It could act as a dagger to our hearts if Moran's men spotted it. Not too soon for my unaccustomed legs, Lauterbrunnen hove into view. The pretty village was tucked into a deep, long valley of rocky cliffs and green pastures. To the left rose the great snow-mountain Jungfrau, towering above the rocky precipices of the Schwarze Mönch. Not far away we could see the Staubbach. Fed by the melting snow its waters tumbled nearly a thousand feet, resembling a silvery veil, wafting to and fro in the breeze. By the time we reached the Hotel Pension Stechtelberg the mountain peaks had begun to cast their evening shadow. The photograph would have to wait for the following day.

I spent much of the next two hours at a vantage point, purporting to survey scenes of interest for postal cards. Anxiously I scanned the track we had taken to the hotel. Colonel Moran's malign presence seemed to envelop the very mountains around us. I had last faced him eleven years earlier, in *The Adventure of the Empty House*. I described him thus: 'one could not look upon his cruel blue eyes, with their drooping, cynical lids, or upon the fierce, aggressive nose and the threatening, deep-lined brow, without reading Nature's plainest danger-signals.'

At a wretchedly early hour we set off, leaving the bicycles at the hotel. The journey to the Trümmelbach was almost entirely uphill. Holmes strode out with the Lancaster's Patent oak and brass tripod while I carried the heavy Sanderson camera. Jutting among the boulders were the descendants of the plants we had trodden on fourteen years before – the large Yellow Vetch, dog's mercury, Star-of-Bethlehem, purple Betony and Giant Ragweed. After frequent stops pretending to survey for a general photographic purpose we arrived at a ledge identical to the one at the Reichenbach Falls.

I set the camera on the tripod and opened the shutter, focusing with the ground glass screen. I had carefully worked out the exposure time and aperture the day before. Holmes watched me fumbling for the exact position for the tripod, edging it as close to the precipice rim as I dared. His lips tightened as the minutes passed. I raised a hand, counted out loud from one to three and operated the shutter. With a click I had the precious plate, my subject suitably bedraggled and grim-visaged. In a few months' time his iconic image would appear on the cover of the *Strand's* bumper Christmas edition.

A second plate was needed to be sure of success. I was about to duck under the black cloth when small particles of rock fell from the cliff above. I threw myself in front of Holmes with as much haste as I could muster on the uneven, soaking ground. I tugged at the revolver in my jacket. My elbow struck the tripod. The apparatus jerked backwards. It seemed to hold at the very edge like a man trying his utmost to stay upright, then the Sanderson toppled into the abyss, taking with it the precious plate. I heard the crack of camera and tripod cannonading from rock to rock.

I stared frantically upward for sight of an enemy. There was no-one to be seen.

'Holmes! Someone is spying on us,' I hissed, uttering the words from the corner of my mouth.

With surprising composure Holmes replied, 'I noticed him too. He has been following us for a while. You may put away your revolver. He is not an assassin.'

Despite my companion's assurance, I kept the revolver pointing at the cliff-face and commanded,

'You, up there. Come out and reveal yourself!'

'You'd best address him by name,' Holmes advised. 'Try "Professor Sobel".'

CHAPTER V

Albert Einstein

Professor Eli Sobel emerged from behind the rock face and scrambled down to join us. 'Gentlemen, I didn't mean to startle you,' he apologised. 'I couldn't approach you at the University among all those people because of the confidential nature of a request I wish to make.' With a diffident look at Holmes, he continued.

'I wouldn't normally ask such a thing of a world-famous sleuthhound but it is a matter of some account to the Physics Department. It concerns a Swiss citizen of German birth; a young physicist at present employed as a technical assistant in the Federal Office for Intellectual Property in Berne.'

'His name?' asked Holmes.

'Albert Einstein. He seeks the post of Lecturer in my Department. The Rector needs to be entirely sure of his good character before we can accept him in the faculty.'

'My dear Professor,' Holmes returned, with the flicker of a frown, 'establishing the *bona fides* of this Albert Einstein seems to me entirely routine. Check with the police or Doctors' Commons or their equivalent wherever he has lived over the past ten years and you have it. I see no difficulty on your part in discovering all you need.'

'I assure you we carried out the usual investigation into the young man, then two mysterious messages in German were sent anonymously to the Rector.'

Our guest thrust a torn piece of paper at us.

69

'Mr. Holmes, I know of your facility with the language. Most of the great works of chemistry are in German. You will have read them in the original. For Dr. Watson's benefit I have put the English translation by its side.'

Written with a sharp pen in red ink the note stated,

> 'A. Einstein is applying for a teaching post at the University. What of Lieserl?'

Holmes looked up at our visitor quizzically.

'What of Lieserl, Professor?'

Professor Sobel shook his head.

'My enquiries have revealed absolutely nothing. It seems to be a Swabian name. Einstein mother was born in the Kingdom of Württemberg, in Swabia, where they speak an Alemannic dialect of High German. I need to discover if the reference to a Lieserl has any importance.'

He fixed my comrade with a beseeching look. 'Mr. Holmes, I would be most grateful if you and Dr. Watson were to take up this matter.'

I intervened. 'What do you know of the lad's private life?'

'Little except that two years ago he married a woman he met at the Zurich *Polytechnikum*. They studied physics together. She's from Serbia.'

'I presume you have brought this note to the young man's attention?' I asked.

The Professor nodded. 'The lad begged me to accept his solemn oath that he knew nothing about a Lieserl.'

'He denied it completely?' Holmes enquired.

'I would apply the word *stürmisch*.'

'Vehemently,' Holmes translated for my benefit.

The Professor reached into a pocket. 'It would all have petered out – but yesterday morning the Rector received the second note.'

Holmes stared at the scrap of paper and passed it on to me. The ragged edge showed it was torn from the first note. In the same red ink and hand it read simply: Titel.

'Titel?' I enquired. 'Is that "title" in English?'

Professor Sobel shrugged. 'Possibly. Or it could refer to an academic degree, *Akademischer Titel*. Or *betiteln* is what you call a nickname. Or it may refer to *Rechtstitel* – legal title. We don't know what it means.'

The Professor pushed his spectacles up on his forehead and stared at Sherlock Holmes.

'These notes have disturbed the Rector, hence my presence here.'

Holmes thought for a while and asked, 'And the name of the woman Einstein married?'

'Family name Marić,' came the reply. 'Mileva Marić. They say she is a genius at mathematics.'

'Do you have any reason to believe Einstein's wife is attempting to thwart his wish to join your Department?' Holmes asked.

'Far from it,' came the emphatic response. 'If those notes are aimed at warning us off Einstein, they cannot be from Mileva. Several weeks ago she sent me a letter. She is manifestly desperate for us to take her husband's ambitions seriously. She says she could even complement his knowledge of physics with her knowledge of mathematics. She outclassed Albert in mathematics at the Polytechnikum.'

He reached into a pocket. 'Mileva enclosed this certificate with the letter to prove her prowess.'

He paused. 'There is one anomalous fact. The same document shows that in 1899 Mileva achieved a 92% mark in physics – exactly the same as Einstein's – yet when the time came to sit her Diplom dissertation she failed twice.'

'When did the second failure occur?' Holmes enquired.

'1901. After that she went back to her parents' home in Novi-Sad.'

'Professor, what of this Einstein? How would you describe him?' I interjected.

'A middle-class Jew. Raised in Ulm and Munich. Something of a loner. In character, brazen beyond his better interests. He wishes to become a member of the Department yet he raises the faculty's hackles by flaunting a taste for flamboyant clothing – typically a sorrel-coloured cape in *le style anglais*, a short top-hat, even an ornate cane. He has high aspirations. The fellow is hardly twenty-five years of age, yet he questions Faraday's law of induction. He failed even to complete his degree at the Munich Luitpold *Gymnasium*. He was unsuccessful in his first go at the entrance exam to the Zurich *Polytechnikum*. When eventually he graduated from the *Polytechnikum* he wasn't hired for an assistantship – the usual course for the School's graduates. His first doctoral thesis was refused. He failed to obtain a teaching post in Switzerland. And despite all this he aspires to tamper with the Laws of Newton.'

'And in his favour?' Holmes asked drily.

The Professor shrugged. 'There is something about this stubborn young man. He could turn out to be a *rara avis* in the world of physics. That's why I want him in my Department. The scientific field is ripe for the emergence of a towering name. Who knows? It could be Einstein.'

Holmes picked up the letter and the document. He stared at them for some moments. To my amazement he said, 'I am inclined to accept the case. There is something perplexing in all this which fascinates me extremely.'

The Professor uttered a sigh of relief. 'I shall, of course, ask the University to cover your expenses, gentlemen, no matter where the trail may take you. Personally, I hope you find nothing more discreditable about the lad than vanity, flat feet and extreme foot perspiration. He wouldn't be the only one with such afflictions in the Physics Department.'

During the walk back down the mountain Professor Sobel offered a suggestion. 'When you are back in Berne go to the Café Bollwerk in the Rotes *Quartier* for lunch. You might get a glance of Einstein there. He leads a company of six young scientists calling themselves the Olympia Academy.'

'How shall we recognise Einstein, what does he look like?' I asked.

'Physically, not tall,' the Professor replied. 'Quite broad shoulders. Light brown complexion. A slight stoop. And a garish black moustache. You can see why Einstein and his colleagues irritate the Rector. In naming themselves the Olympia Academy they deliberately mock the official bodies that dominate science. The Bollwerk is where the "Academicians" sometimes gather around noon. At the very least you might bump into his colleague from the Federal Patents Office, a Michele Besso.'

I asked him, 'Tell me, Professor, how did you know we would be at the Trümmelbach and not the Reichenbach Falls?'

'Elementary, my dear Watson,' Professor Sobel replied, smiling. 'As soon as I read the *Journal de Genève* I realised you would have to make yourselves scarce, but I knew Mr. Holmes would never flee without completing your mission. I merely had to look on the map for a similar waterfall.'

Some distance short of our hotel the Professor took his leave. As he did so he called back, 'Mr. Holmes, young Einstein's fate lies entirely in your hands.'

***

'Watson,' Holmes remarked suddenly, 'We shall take the Professor's advice and visit the Café Bollwerk. Serbia lies on our horizon. We can donate our bicycles to the Olympia Academy. I would rather ride a mustang backwards, chased by scalp-hungry Sioux Indians, than pedal the wretched things through the baking plains of Serbia or the mountains of Montenegro.'

One of Sherlock Holmes's defects—if, indeed, one may call it a defect—is his unwillingness to communicate his full plans to any other person until the instant of their fulfilment.

'Serbia, Holmes?' I spluttered. 'If I am to be frank with you, there is nothing in this matter for us. There isn't a man at Scotland Yard, from the oldest inspector to the youngest constable, who wouldn't reject this case out of hand. This is hardly another summons to Odessa as in the case of the Trepoff murder, it equates more to giving advice to distressed governesses.'

I continued in full flow. 'Besides, I can't see how I can entice the editor of the *Strand* into publishing an enquiry into the internal matters of a university Physics Department. What is there here to fascinate my readers? Where is murder, conspiracy, betrayal, to feed their hunger? Can you imagine the schoolmaster, the doctor, the tradesman, solicitor, engineer, each clamouring at the railway bookstalls to buy a copy for the long journey home, only to discover a narrative about a Swabian Jew and his sweaty feet?'

My indignation mounted. 'More to the point, we're hardly likely to become rich beyond the dreams of Croesus. There isn't even a payment! What's more, I have lost my fee for the photograph.'

Holmes looked at me, unable to suppress a smile. 'I hold there is more to this present case than we can possibly know, Watson. The second note. Doesn't it indicate a very pretty little mystery?'

'Titel?' I queried.

'Cast your mind back, Watson, to the time the Prince Regnant of Bulgaria asked us to change to second class carriages at Marchegg. Did you fail to note the instruction on one of the destination boards, 'For Titel take the service to Novi-Sad/Újvidék'?'

'Holmes!' I exploded. 'I'd have thought our time in Bulgaria was enough experience of the Balkans for any one life-time – once again we shall be in shot-and-powder country. If we suspect a jilted woman, why not here in Berne - or Zurich where Einstein spent so much time? By summer the whole of Serbia will be a boiling cauldron of disease. I invite you to take your pick of which pestilence you'd most like to send us to a premature grave. If malaria fails to harm us, there's always typhus, cholera, measles and chicken-pox just over the horizon. Balkan rat fleas still carry the *Yersinia pestis* bacterium which causes the Black Death. By comparison the ravages of diphtheria in Birmingham in the 1870s will be as nothing.'

Holmes's mouth twitched in a slight smile. 'My dear Watson, whoever wrote those notes to Professor Sobel has decided we would be wasting our time anywhere but Serbia. At the very least Titel will take us far from Colonel Moran and his men. For a while longer you must suppress your desire for the amiable Mrs. Hudson's green peas each evening at 7.30 sharp.'

He went on, 'Did you notice the type of paper the notes were written on?'

'Not especially. Only that it wasn't Bohemian paper. As I recall, it was unbleached and similar to hard antique paper.'

'Good, Watson. The paper is much too sturdy for normal correspondence. Given your time in Afghanistan with the Berkshires I'm surprised you failed to make more of it. I shall forgive you because such paper is no longer used by the major Powers for the tube section of shot-shells, but such paper still continues to be used for encasing ammunition in the Balkans.'

'Of course!' I exclaimed. 'Cartridge paper!'

'As to the cover role we should adopt,' Holmes continued, 'now that you are without a camera, the same attire will do perfectly well for an angler. I shall ask Mycroft to go to Hardy's and arrange for a pair of ferruled fly rods to be delivered to us under assumed names, one for salmon, the other a single-handed for trout. I shall also request a collection of James Gregory lures and some flies. How about Mr. W. Senior's Red Spinners on a Snecky Limerick grilse hook? For cloudy days this fly should, I think, be dressed with a dark shade of tinsel and the *coch-y-bondu* hackle. What d'you say?'

My jaw dropped. Where had Homes picked up so much angling knowledge? Not once had I seen him on a river-bank, rod to hand.

**

That night I lay in bed retracing my steps during long-gone days and nights. The Alps triggered memories of the mountain ranges of Afghanistan in 1880 on the eve of the Battle of Maiwand. I recalled in vivid detail my first night sleeping under the stars. The rustle of trees. The hump-backed moon. The alarms and excursions, rumour and counter-rumour. Heliographs flashing in the rising sun. The crackle of Martini rifles.

I relived our punitive expedition's early morning marches across rickety bridges over mountain streams to reach the Pass and confront Ayub Khan before he could lead his men a final fifty miles south-east to Candahar. Rumour circulated that St. Petersburg had supplied Ayub Khan with three thousand Turcoman cavalry. The rattle of our Gardner guns echoed Ayub's superior Nordenfelts. Attack and counter-attack, cold then hot. The slaughter. The terrible heat. Suddenly, astonishingly, the galloper clattering up with the shout, *'Sauve qui peut.'*

The rout was over. We had lost what we had expected to be one of the lesser hill wars. Out of the Brigade's two-and-a-half thousand brave soldiers almost a thousand lay dead. The wounded endured the nightmare journey to a line of hospitals in Peshawar and Rawal Pindi, Deolali and Nowshera, where cholera awaited them. Young Rudyard Kipling later wrote of the battle:

There was thirty dead an' wounded on the ground we
wouldn't keep –
No, there wasn't more than twenty when the front
began to go –
But, Christ! along the line o' flight they cut us up like
sheep,
An' that was all we gained by doing so.

I thought of the rotting, uncoffined bodies of the dead in the
mortuary tents. I thought more cheerfully of Bobbie, the
regimental mascot, wounded like me at Maiwand, but able to
make his way back unaided to his kennel at the fort, to die many
happy years later, safe in England's bosom. The campaign had
brought promotion and honours to many, but for my Army
career it had nothing but misfortune. With a shoulder wound,
my time in the East had come to its end.

***

In the morning a dog-cart bearing the insignia of the Swiss Post
clattered up to the Hotel Pension Stechtelberg. It brought the
fishing equipment sent by the assiduous Mycroft. He had
included a brand-new copy of Philip Geen's *What I Have Seen
While Fishing and How I Have Caught My Fish*. The Angling
guide was accompanied by a slip with the author's scribbled
words: 'Dr. Watson. From the President of the London Anglers.
See you at Euston Jan. 14. Bring Lob worms. Long live shoals
of 3lb roach'.

I had met the grand old salmon-fisher some years before
when I set out to entice Holmes to follow in Boswell's and Dr.
Johnson's footsteps through the Highlands and Western Isles.

Instead, Holmes had turned the proposed fishing trip to Scotland into an opportunity to rid himself of my company for a while. I found myself companionless in the smoking saloon of a sleeping-car, surrounded by a merry and boisterous crew of gentlemen, anglers all. They suffered from the insidious malady my medical skills could never remedy, spring salmon fever.

Chapter VI

We Meet Mileva

Our bicycles took us through Berne's narrow streets, past sandstone facades, fountains and historic towers to the Café Bollwerk. A waiter led us to a vacant table at the café's outermost circle. We sat among solid burghers of *Mitteleuropa* in linen suits and Leghorn straw hats. The air was rank with the highly scented tobacco smoked incessantly by gaggles of talkative students. We had been there ten minutes when a young man of open countenance came towards us and greeted us.

'I'm Michele Besso. I heard from Professor Sobel that you would be here. He mentioned you are very kindly donating your beautiful bicycles to the Olympia academicians.'

He continued, 'Would it be all right if I sit with you for a while? I so wanted to meet you, Mr. Holmes.'

We called a waiter and ordered coffee. Holmes said, 'I observe from your forefinger that you make your own cigarettes. Have no hesitation in lighting one,' at which our young visitor drew out paper and tobacco and twirled the one up in the other with great dexterity.

'I hear you're a close colleague of Einstein?' I put encouragingly.

'At the Patent Office they call us the Eagle and the Sparrow,' he agreed, adding with a rueful laugh, 'I hardly need to tell you which of us is the sparrow.'

He lit the cigarette and continued, 'Mr. Holmes, I have heard you are something of an expert on the causes of the change in the obliquity of the ecliptic. Perhaps you can give us some advice. Albert and I are trying to solve a problem that's been discussed for more than fifty years, the anomalous advance of Mercury's perihelion. We have checked whether other theories – Henri Poincaré's especially, or those of Minkowski, Abraham or Nordström – can account for the Mercury anomaly. None of them can.' He added, 'Had you not disposed of Professor Moriarty, Albert and I may well have consulted him on the matter.'

A young woman with a slight limp wended her way through the crowded tables towards us. She wore an orthopaedic shoe on her left foot. A sleeping infant was tied to her, peasant style, by a shawl. Besso stood up.

'Mileva!' he called to her with a welcoming gesture. '*Wir sind hier!*'

He formally introduced the newcomer to us as Albert Einstein's wife, Mileva Marić-Einstein.

'And who is this?' I asked, pointing to the child.

'This is Hans Albert,' Mileva replied, laughing at my polite interest. 'He's our first son.'

'We all call him *Steinli*,' Besso remarked. 'It means 'Little Stone'.'

The new arrival broke into a pleasing smile at the mention of her child's nickname.

I studied Mileva as closely as I dared without being impolite. She wore a soft white cotton shirtwaist with a high lace collar. The nose was small and turned up, her hair pinned up loosely in a chignon. The large black eyes portrayed an intense intelligence. With her came the sweet and pungent odour of Tamjan, produced by the sap of the Bosuellia plant. It was a scent I remembered from our visit to the Balkans five years earlier.

She glanced around eagerly to see if her husband was on the point of arriving. Failing to see him she remained standing, looking down at Besso, a hand on his shoulder. He remarked,

'Mileva, you're looking very satisfied with yourself.'

'I am, Michele,' came the reply.

'Because?' Besso prodded.

'You'll see. Soon Albert will publish a paper that will make him world famous.'

'How soon?' Besso asked.

'Soon enough,' came the reply. With one more glance around the café she prepared to leave.

'*Meine Herren*, I can't stay. Michele, can you give Albert a message? Tell him he'll be happy to know Rózsika returns to Novi-Sad tonight.'

She indicated a young untidy-looking woman staring in our direction. Mileva's voice dropped. 'My sister Rózsika comes to stay with us once in a while. Albert doesn't find her very – *gemütlich*.'

Mileva went on, 'My sister's not very sociable. She refuses to join in.'

The sibling rested on a leg which also ended in an orthopaedic shoe. I knew from our visit to Serbia's neighbour Bulgaria that such deformation of the hip ran widely in the Balkans. Unkindly, it had affected both sisters.

Mileva bade us goodbye.

83

'The younger sister,' Besso said, with sympathy in his voice. 'Albert will be cheered by the news of her departure. They say the fairies brought Rózsika an illegitimate daughter, but soon they took it away. Albert says she makes his skin crawl just by her presence, but he can't stop her visits. Mileva likes to catch up on all the news from home.'

'Tell us about Mileva,' I urged.

'She adores Albert beyond measure,' Besso responded. 'Last week I observed her catching sight of his back in the distance. Her face lit up. Never has a single look demonstrated such a womanly love as I saw then. She puts Albert's career success infinitely ahead of her own. It's an irony that at one time she might have had a better chance than Albert in gaining employment at the University. Her grades in physics and mathematics at the Royal Classical High School in Zagreb were the highest ever awarded. Her teachers wrote the word 'brilliant' on her report.'

His brow wrinkled. 'Which makes what happened later the odder.'

'Odder?' I queried, my sympathy and curiosity alerted in equal measures.

'Nine years ago she was admitted to the Physics Department of the Zurich *Polytechnikum*. She was only the fifth woman admitted to the Department and without doubt the first Serb. She studied not only theoretical physics, applied physics, and experimental physics but also differential and integral calculus, descriptive and projective geometry, plus mechanics and astronomy.'

He glanced around to be sure Mileva was out of ear-shot.

'She was working on her dissertation on the topic of thermo-conduction when suddenly, around October 1901, she drops out. Without offering even friends like me an explanation, she returns to her family in Novi-Sad. She remains there out of sight, doing nothing, for many, many months until she comes back to Berne to marry Albert.'

Besso described how, when Mileva was away in Serbia, Einstein worked day after day on the metric field describing space and time for a rotating observer. 'He encountered mathematical difficulties quite beyond his ability to conquer. Time and again he shouted at me he was going crazy. He is certain that gravity and acceleration are one and the same thing. One day he came rushing over to see me. He was sure he had solved the problem.'

Besso shrugged expressively. 'You can't come up with such an idea without good mathematical reasoning, but Albert is Albert. He was so convinced he had the answer he put his theory in an envelope to send to the *Annalen der Physik*. Luckily Mileva came back just in time. She found he'd made a trivial mistake. Both the energy of the point mass *and the energy of the metric field* must be taken into account.'

He smiled. 'Without Mileva, Albert would have become a laughing stock. Anything he turned out afterwards would have been scorned. For the moment he has given up on these field equations but I know he and Mileva have been working on something else of the greatest importance.'

Holmes was silent, but little darting glances showed me the interest he took in our companion.

Besso leaned forward.

'People say her mathematics is why Albert married Mileva. Why else? they say. They point to the club foot and the grating Novi-Sad accent. But she is a wonder on the *tamburitzsa* and when she plays Brahms on the piano, ah! It's like an angel from Heaven has taken control of the keys.'

Besso paused. 'Mileva has such a happy personality she inspires her friends with happiness too. At least that was so until some little while ago.'

'At which point?' I prompted.

'Her mood changed. Something must have happened at that time. In 1903. Yes. Around September. They'd been married about eight months. I can't explain it any other way than that she stopped smiling. In some way she seems to be holding Albert responsible for whatever happened. One day she was so alive – the next, visibly distraught. For a while she even stopped coming to the Olympia Academy.'

He gave us an unhappy look.

'She has stayed that way to this day. The only time she has warmth in her smile is when she speaks of Steinli, her little Hans. I am not the only person to notice it,' he added. 'We all have.'

He caught my quizzical look, and went on, 'We tried. I asked Mileva more than once. She would say only it was "intensely personal". Whatever it was, she has gone on brooding ever since.'

He squinted up at a clock-tower. 'Albert won't be coming now. I must return to my lectern. Albert calls it "our cobbler's trade": 3,500 Swiss francs a month is not the highest salary in the world, but it gets me by!'

86

Besso stood up and thanked us for the bicycles. He led them away as a man would lead two purebred Arab stallions into the enclosure.

'Albert and I will make excellent use of these wonderful creatures,' he called back.

We sat for a while after Besso's departure. With no sign of Albert Einstein we left the café and hailed a motorised taxicab to take us via a circuitous route back to the Hotel Sternen Muri. In the cab Holmes pulled the note with the word *Titel* from his pocket and examined it, brow furrowed.

'I deduce from the handwriting that the author is female and young,' he said. 'I would not vouchsafe her equilibrium. See the extreme height differentials – and how strikingly the words slant to the left. Look at the strange ending of letters. The 'ts' – the capital 'T' and the middle 't'. They are vigorously crossed. It can only imply the highest possibility of impetuous violence.'

I looked across at Holmes affectionately. Only disciples of water-divining, spiritualism, socialism, fortune-telling, naturism and animal magnetism made as many claims as graphologists.

Holmes went on, 'Before I forget, Watson, there is a little masquerade I wish you to undertake here in Berne. Let's discuss it to-morrow.'

The next day, I entered the hotel breakfast room. Before I could greet him with a customary good morning, Holmes met me with my instructions.

'I need you to look your most respectable and walk into the bank nearest Einstein's address on the Tillierstrasse. It's called the Spar Leihkasse. Demand to see your bank-statements – that is, Albert Einstein's bank statements. A bank has a thousand customers a day. It's hardly likely any teller would know the real Einstein from the ghost of Newton.'

'Why would you wish to know how much this young man has in his bank-account? It can hardly be the equal of Baron de Rothschild,' I demanded.

'Not so much his financial standing, but the manner of his outlays,' came the explanation. 'I can tell eighty percent of a man's secrets from one glance at his accounts. What of regular payments of a precise amount over many months or years? Landlord? Mistress? Blackmailer?'

'Holmes,' I protested, 'other than greatly inadequate French and a smattering of Urdu in which Swiss bank tellers may have little grounding, I speak only English!'

'My dear fellow, look how the students around us at the Café Bollwerk converse – English is the *lingua franca*. Einstein is a Jew, born in Bavaria. His native tongue would be a colloquial German, but it is quite likely he would use English at a bank.'

Despite my evident discomfort at the task, I was dismissed with a 'Good-bye and be brave, Watson – it's hardly a case of performing the triple somersault.'

I entered the Bank with a show of confidence I didn't feel. If the teller shouted out for my arrest, my advancing years and stiffening limbs would make an escape to the outside world difficult. The teller greeted me politely with a *'Comment puis-je vous aider, Monsieur?'*

In English I replied, 'I wish to see my bank-statements for the last three months of 1904.'

'Certainly, sir,' came the reply in English. 'Your name, please?'

'Mr. Albert Einstein,' I replied.

He began writing 'Albert' then stopped, looking up at me over his eyeglasses.

'Albert –?'

'Einstein,' I responded firmly.

'Did you say Albert Einstein?'

'Yes,' I repeated stoutly. 'Mr. Albert Einstein of the Tillierstrasse.'

'The Tillierstrasse?' he parroted.

'Yes, the Tillierstrasse,' I returned, trying to look suitably bewildered and irritated by this interrogation.

The Bank teller leaned towards me.

'I have a reason for asking you to repeat your name. You see, ever since the Great Council of Geneva in 1713 we are prohibited from revealing details about our customers to anyone else but the account holder.'

'Such discretion is the hallmark of the Spar Leihkasse Bank and the principal reason I bank with you,' I retorted. 'I am a customer and my name is Albert Einstein.'

A smile crept across his face. He turned to a small notebook at his side. From it he wrote on a piece of scrap paper what appeared to be a telephone number and slipped it through the grill.

'What's this?' I asked, bewildered.

'Our famous University's Medical Department,' came the reply.

'Why should I want – ?'

His smile broadened. 'Mr. Albert Einstein, I must ask you to offer yourself as a guinea-pig in the University's Gerontology department.'

'Why in Heaven's name would I do that?' I protested.

'Because in hardly three hours, you have aged more than thirty years. You were here this morning exactly where you stand before me, trying to get the bank to increase your overdraft. If indeed you're the same Albert Einstein you really must avoid repeating whatever it was you ate for lunch.'

He sat back on his uncomfortable stool. 'I realise you may be one of Mr. Einstein's many creditors, *Mein Herr*, but I must wish you good-day before I call the police and have you questioned in some depth.'

I hurried out of the bank, relieved at avoiding a confrontation with the Berne police. Holmes waved at me from a horse cab across the busy street. I started to cross towards him. As I did so, my attention was caught by a large brass and mahogany Thornton Pickard half-plate bellows camera on a tripod. The operator was hidden beneath the black cloth, turning a handle which moved the lens back and forth. The camera was focusing on the upper floors of the Spar Leihkasse bank. A hand with a large Jerusalem cross tattooed across the fingers reached out to pull the tripod back a foot. I had last seen that tattoo on the hand of a bank-robber in the case of the Red-Headed League. Inspector Lestrade of the Yard described the robber, John Clay, as 'the fourth cleverest man in London - I've been on his track for years. Despite the tattoo I've never set eyes on him yet.' Police agent Jones told me, 'John Clay, bank-robber and forger. He's a young man but he is at the head of his profession, and I would rather have my bracelets on him than on any criminal in London.'

I signalled to Holmes, making a covert gesture towards the photographer. Holmes understood at once. He descended from the cab and walked quietly up to the man crouching behind the camera. With a rapid movement he pulled away the cloth. It revealed the astonished face of John Clay.

'Mr. Clay,' Holmes said, 'we meet again.'

Chapter VII

We Plunge into Serbia

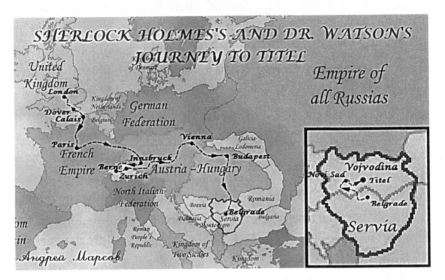

I pondered on what our next move would be. Holmes settled the matter. He announced we would take the morning train to Serbia.

'Surely, Holmes,' I protested, 'we must first start our investigations here in Berne, or in Swabia?'

'You would be quite mistaken to do so, Watson,' my comrade replied. 'If just the one note had been sent, we would have started in Switzerland or Germany. The second note told us that if anything was to be uncovered about Einstein it would be in Serbia. It pointed us to Titel but we shall need to start our search in Novi-Sad. Novi-Sad is the regional centre. That's where all the records will be held. We may after all need my brother Mycroft's involvement to find our way through officialdom.'

The early-morning express came roaring into the station. We boarded it, our first stop Zurich, then beyond to Vienna and onward into the Balkans. Thirty-six hours later we arrived in Novi-Sad, a medium-sized town set among acacia trees at the foot of the Fruška Gora hills. The upper slopes were covered with dense deciduous forests, providing shelter for deer, jackals, boar and lynx. Our Baedeker told us Novi-Sad itself was home to Hungarians, Germans, Croats, Slovaks, Ruthenians, Greeks, Cincars, Jews, Romanians and Roma. Above, on the right bank of the Danube River, loomed the great Petrovaradin Fortress constructed three hundred years earlier at the 1244th kilometre of the River Danube's course. Our carriage dropped us at the Hotel Tvrdjava Leopold I, a Renaissance building near the Varadin Bridge.

Holmes was clearly impatient at breakfast. The expected communication from his brother Mycroft had not arrived. Without it we were powerless to start our enquiries. No government employee in this vast and bureaucratic Austro-Hungarian Empire would allow us access to municipal records without proper permissions, in triplicate probably, and stamped with many seals. I suggested we start by purchasing a map of Novi-Sad.

Before Holmes could reply, a crowd of hotel guests flocked into the breakfast room. The tables around us buzzed with life. Teutonic voices filled the air. I questioned the waiter. He explained it was a fishing competition. More than thirty German anglers came down every year at this time to fish on the Franz Joseph Canal, a waterway famed for its variety and quantity of fish – bream, roach, rudd, Prussian carp, bighead carp, perch, pike, and cat-fish.

One of the anglers at the next table heard my question. In excellent English he called over, 'Gentlemen, we have rented thirty-two fishing spots, but one of our members couldn't come. One of you is welcome to join us.'

I looked eagerly at Holmes. He waved a hand graciously.

'My dear Watson, who am I to stand in your way when it comes to fishing?'

My new host introduced himself as Dr. Herdlitzschke, a specialist in contagious diseases. He himself was resident in Novi-Sad. He would supply the spare seat, fish keeping net and fish bait.

'Dr. Watson,' I returned. 'I too am a medical man, in London.'

I handed him my visiting card with the Junior United Service Club address and took his. It was eight o'clock. The charabanc would leave in an hour.

***

My new fishing companion Dr. Herdlitzschke settled me at a neighbouring peg on the canal bank. He informed me that he came from southern Germany.

'From Bavarian Swabia. We have a joke about ourselves. We say *"Wir können alles. Außer Hochdeutsch"*. In English it means "We can do everything—except speak Standard German".'

At this very spot, he told me, he had once caught 129 fishes with a float and one hook in a single day, mostly roach and rudd. He had heard of extraordinary catches on the Tisza - cat-fish weighing 90 kilogrammes, and river char at more than 30 kilogrammes. In the lakes there were brown trout above 25 kilogrammes. He asked why I was in Novi-Sad. Was it in a professional capacity? His own hospital was staffed more by foreign doctors than Serbians. With the advent of summer he always had room for one more.

'No,' I replied, 'something quite different. My colleague Sherlock Holmes and I are searching for someone. A woman.'

'Sherlock Holmes!' he exclaimed. 'So you are *the* Dr. Watson!'

I nodded, flattered.

'The name of the woman you seek?'

'Lieserl,' I replied, uncertain of the pronunciation. 'L-i-e-s-e-r-l.'

'Lieserl?' he repeated. 'Where I come from we have lots of Lieserls but none of them is strictly speaking likely to be a woman.'

I stared at him in astonishment.

'Not a woman?' I exclaimed.

'Not exactly,' he affirmed. 'In Swabian, the 'er' in "Lieserl" describes definitely an infant. Like Büberl or Mäderl. Something very small. Very rarely would we use such an endearment for an adult woman.'

***

Holmes and I were settling into breakfast at the hotel when a boy in uniform brought an envelope to our table marked SECRET, PERSONAL, ADDRESSEE'S EYES ONLY. It was from Holmes's brother Mycroft.

As from No. 10, Downing Street.

96

Dear Sherlock,

His Majesty's Ambassador in Vienna has arranged for you to inspect the records at the Novi-Sad Town Hall. Take with you the credentials contained in this letter. You may well encounter certain difficulties in pursuing your Balkan searches. I sympathise. You would not be the first to come away from those pocket handkerchief states heartsick and humbled. The Balkan States have endured centuries of misrule under Ottoman Absolutist regimes whose functionaries are a byword for injustice and malpractice. It is a constant stimulus for revolutionary activity. The Peninsular may be separated from the rest of Europe solely by the width of the Danube and the narrowness of the Straits of Otranto, but we know as little of it as we do of the industrious navigators digging the canals of Mars.

I suggest a meeting with a Miss Edith Durham could be helpful in your quest. She is an Englishwoman, font of much knowledge of the region. She is staying for a few days at the Vaskrsenja Hristova Monastery near Kać, ostensibly to study local traditions and to make drawings of amphibia. Miss Durham alone is at liberty to tell you the real reason for her presence. It is enough for me to say that England takes its holdings in and around the eastern Mediterranean very seriously.

I have asked Miss Durham to remain at the Monastery until you arrive.

Mycroft.

I then revealed my discovery. 'Holmes,' I chided, 'how is it you didn't know Lieserl could only apply to a small child?'

'My dear Watson,' came the answer. 'I'd have been quicker off the mark if my Cambridge tutor had been born in Stuttgart rather than in Hanover where they speak High German. Swabian was as alien to him as Broad Yorkshire with its roots in Old Norse is to you and me. He knew one word in the dialect, *Präschtlingsgsälz*, as unpronounceable a word to most Germans as Shakespeare's *honorificabilitudinitatibus* is to us.'

'And therefore a word of some importance, I presume…the Swabian word means?' I enquired.

'Strawberry jam.'

Armed with our new knowledge and the impressive document with its multiple seals we set off for the Town Hall, an imposing building on the north side of the central square. The next two days were spent browsing through municipal and census records under the eye of a watchful civil servant. Nowhere was the name 'Liese' or 'Lieserl' mentioned in connection with the surnames Marić, Marity, Mariti, Einstein, Ajnštajn or Ružić. The evening of the second day approached. The clerk had been assiduous in pulling out ledgers but we had discovered nothing. We showed our appreciation with a *thaler* and began to walk in despondent mood back to our lodgings. At some distance from the Town Hall we heard the footsteps of someone hurrying to catch up with us. It was the same clerk.

'You will learn nothing about the Marić family from official records,' he said. 'Miloš Marić's tentacles stretch into every corner. He knows everyone. He has been an official at district courts in Ruma and Vukovar and appointed to the High Court in Zagreb. He owns a great deal of property – three farms in Banja

Luka and large homes in Titel, Novi-Sad and Kać. He is still an official in Novi-Sad's Serbian Reading Room. No civil servant or cleric would spread gossip about Marić or his family for fear of their livelihood.'

'What do you suggest?' I asked.

In a near whisper he added, 'There is someone who might help you with the information you seek. My cousin. Her name's Jelena. Jelena's mother-in-law is a friend, but not a blood relative, of the Marić family, not a *porodica*,' he explained. 'This puts her distant enough not to feel her lips completely sealed yet close enough to have heard any gossip. I can arrange for you to meet her.'

A message was delivered to our hotel later that evening. We were to rendezvous with Jelena at the Queen Elizabeth Café.

***

We entered the café at the arranged hour. A woman with thick grey hair trimmed short beckoned us. She was seated at a tiny marble-topped table set among potted white lilacs. Slavonic grey eyes in an oval-shaped face watched us carefully as we approached. In accented English she acknowledged the Swiss chocolates we placed before her.

'I heard about your search,' she commenced. She produced a tiny white fluted teacup and placed it on the table.

'This teacup – it's the one Albert always requests when he comes to my home for tea.' She added, apropos of nothing, 'It was Albert who designed the *ulaz za mačku* – a cat entrance for my Milica.'

My hopes rose. If we were to discover any link to the mysterious Lieserl, surely it would be from such an intimate source as the woman seated before us. 'What can you tell us about Mileva?' I asked.

Jelena planted her elbows on the table. 'The woman is a mathematical genius. Her father Miloš encouraged her to study the subject for a good reason,' she added, now looking down at her hands.

'For what reason?' I prompted.

'For the obvious reason she would need a profession, a teacher,' the woman snapped. Her tone was spiteful.

'If Mileva had stayed in Serbia she would have stayed a spinster for ever. In the Vojvodina culture we consider a woman like Mileva completely unmarriageable.'

She gave what sounded like a snort of contempt. 'She is ugly. Mileva would never have found anyone to marry her. It is a fact,' she added conclusively.

Her eyes darted up from her hands and fixed on Holmes.

'Perhaps you can explain to me why this Einstein married her. After all, he is a German and Germans consider Slavs backward. He is a Jew and Jews marry into their own. She's four years older than her husband. Marrying a woman several years older is a Serbian custom but it is not a German one.' She added, 'And she's a cripple.'

Her cold stare shifted across to me. 'Why do you think the Jew married her?' she asked.

I indicated I had no idea.

'I could tell you,' she went on.

I took a sovereign from my pocket and pushed it discreetly to her.

'The reason is simple,' she retorted, 'and unarguable.'

She placed the coin carefully in her purse. 'Because she gave the young Jew presents!'

'Presents?' I echoed.

'Gifts.'

'What sort of gifts?' Holmes asked.

'Shirts.'

I was confounded by this trivial revelation. Was this some Balkan equivalent of a dowry?

'Shirts?' I repeated.

In a high-pitched voice she burst out with two lines of a song, and translated them – spitting the words at us: '"In Banok and Bjelopavlice – she called to everyone. To everyone she gave a shirt".'

Heads swung round. Jelena's grey eyes turned almost black. With an abrupt movement she stood up, the chair scraping away from the table.

She said in a harsh tone, 'I have work to do. You must excuse me. I have told you everything I wish to. We have a saying *zaklela se zemlja raju da se tajne sve saznaju* – the Earth pledged to Paradise that all secrets will be revealed. May you have a pleasant stay in my country and a safe return journey to your homeland.'

The meeting had come to an abrupt and disturbing end.

Over dinner at the hotel I looked at Holmes despondently.

'A shirt,' I repeated. 'We don't seem to be getting anywhere, do we?'

'There are certainly difficulties,' Holmes agreed. 'We are in the Balkans, dear fellow. We must conduct our affairs according to the precept of the Iron Duke – the whole art of war consists of guessing what's at the other side of the hill. And now, my dear

Watson, since the official records reveal nothing, we must look elsewhere.'

I reminded him that Dr. Herdlitzschke had suggested a check of hospital records. An exceptionally virulent Scarlet Fever epidemic had ravaged the region in the summer of 1903. Four hundred of Novi-Sad's one thousand children died from that cause alone that year. The Doctor had patrolled hospital wards crammed with dead or dying children, their pulses racing, tongues bright strawberry red, and throats a deep crimson.

Another day dawned. We left the hotel and hailed a cab. I showed the cabbie the address of the section for children's contagious diseases at the Hospital St. László. As I sank back with relief in the familiar cool interior of a Hansom cab, I remarked,

'What would we do without the Hansom! They say there are 7500 of them in London alone, and many more in Paris, Berlin, St Petersburg and New York.'

Holmes grunted. At the St. László two bored-looking hospital receptionists barely raised their heads at our arrival. Thirty seconds passed in silence, forty, then fifty. One minute. Two. Holmes fingered a Maria Theresa *thaler*. The heavy coin had an electrifying effect. What was it we wished to know? An animated conversation between the women ensued, to no avail. Some of the records had gone up in flames a few days before. We could try elsewhere, for example the Rókus Kórház, the hospital for poor people. It included a children's wing for contagious diseases. We discovered nothing there either.

Noting our frustration, the staff at the Rókus Kórház suggested our inability to find any information on this Lieserl might mean she was born 'Stupid'. There was a special place for

102

such luckless creatures, the *Orságes Pszichiátria es Neurológia Intezet*, the State Asylum.

The walls of the *Orságes Pszichiátria's* dim corridors were crumbling, the floors dirty and cracked. Large damp patches threatened to bring down the ceiling. The stench of mildew was overpowering. The production of another *thaler* led us to the inner sanctum which turned out to be a dank cellar scattered with crates of old case records and a box of photographs.

A listless woman clerk with long black hair and kohl eyeliner pulled out a large, leather-bound ledger listing female patients for the last seven years. The book contained thirteen names, date of arrival, condition (mostly 'stupidity', 'severe stupidity' or 'mongoloid idiot'), date of departure or, more often, 'Discharged Dead'. But – no mention of a Lieserl. The clerk closed the sad book. She advised us to pursue our quest among the records at the Wolf Valley Cemetery in District X11.

This time we waved down a *Fijaker*. The black leather top smelt of the cow it had been until recently. At the cemetery, an elderly gravedigger told us that if graves were not paid for year by year, the remains were exhumed and placed in a nearby charnel house or disposed of in a garbage heap. Yes, he had dug up and thrown a lot of children's bones on the heap. Were there any headstones with the name Lieserl? He shrugged. Gravestones for children were not the custom in Serbia. Unchristened children were put in a box and buried at the edge of the cemetery. Sometimes there would be small wooden crosses but they disintegrated after one or two severe winters.

'You might go to see Father Magyar,' he advised. 'He is a priest of the Orthodox Church. He has records of adoptions and children with disabilities.' The grave-digger accepted a coin

103

gratefully and resumed work on an infant's half-dug grave, already fourth in line marked out of a further two dozen or more.

The visit to Father Magyar proved equally fruitless. We heard then that a long-standing girlfriend of Mileva called Desana Tapavica was now married to a Dr. Emil Bala, Novi-Sad's mayor. The mayor received us and told us nothing. The wife refused to meet us. I paid for a search through *Politika* and other Serbian newspapers. More days passed. We were told Lieserl was the name of an infant who had been christened in the ancient Kovilj Monastery situated between Novi-Sad and Titel. To get to the monastery we bumped along dusty, deeply rutted roads, among pale ochre houses with lace-curtained windows and brown wooden shutters. Despite spending hours with a monk, searching through every record in the archives, we found nothing. In this strange Serbian world we were out of our depth. Holmes became more and more terse. At home in England, among the coiners and smashers and cheque sharps of London's underworld, my comrade's every word, every glance, suggested he knew something you didn't, some secret which would give him the eternal upper hand – but here, in the Balkans...

We had arranged for our post to await collection at the principal Post Office. The sole letter was from the bank robber John Clay. He mockingly signed himself with the initials of his former alias, Vincent Spaulding.

'Berne. Mission successful. Two regular outgoing payments appear on A. Einstein's accounts, to proprietor of house on Tillierstrasse and to M. Maritsch-Einstein. No further such payments. V.S.'

There was a Postscript: 'No need to remit fee – the Spar Leihkasse Bank has paid generously on your behalf.'

The Tillierstrasse payments were presumably the rent. Housekeeping costs would account for the payments to Albert Einstein's wife. We left the Post Office and returned to the hotel.

'Watson,' Holmes mused, 'we find a world of strange anomalies and questionable clues. We reach. We grasp. What is left in our hands at the end? A shadow. The more we investigate the details and circumstances, the more inexplicable they become. We must work on the supposition that this Lieserl is a child and that she is connected in some way to Einstein. Despite all our efforts we have been unable to discover anything about her – no legal papers, no family papers such as a baptismal certificate, no death certificate, no other customary civic record. How can this be? Every detail of every Serb from birth to death is minutely recorded and stored – in doctors' offices, town halls, churches, monasteries, synagogues, yet not one document concerning a Lieserl exists. Why the lack even of a birth certificate?'

With frustration in his voice he continued. 'In a world so filled with officials and paper, do we assume there never was a Lieserl?'

I remained silent. I knew from lengthy experience that Holmes was in no way asking my opinion on the matter.

'Or is someone a step ahead of us at every turn. If so – why?'

He stood up with a clouded brow and went to the window. The lights were coming on in Novi-Sad.

'The word 'Titel' brought us to Serbia to make a search for Lieserl,' he mused. 'We are in a town in a region where rumour-mongering is a way of life, yet whenever we enquire about Lieserl every door slams, every voice abruptly stills. So far we have been offered three theories. Dr. Herdlitzschke suggested Lieserl might have died in the 1903 epidemic of scarlet fever. Death certificates exist for every one of four hundred child victims but not for a Lieserl. The Rókus Kórház hinted without any evidence that the infant might have been sent to another village for adoption, a concept entirely repugnant to a self-respecting family. The monk at the Kovilj monastery suggested she might have been packed off to an institution for imbecilic infants. Yet from Clay's inspection of Einstein's bank account, there is no evidence that he makes more than the two regular payments, to the landlord and to Mileva for household matters, neither to an adoptive family nor to a home for mongoloid children.'

Holmes turned back from the window. 'All we can say is that if there is a connection between Einstein and Lieserl, every effort has been made by public officials, priests, monks, friends, family and relatives by marriage, to seek out and destroy every document with the child's name on it. The question is – why?'

He paused. 'Either we go on striving like the Old Man in *Alice*, to "madly squeeze a right-hand foot into a left-hand shoe", or – '

In gloomy silence we ate a dinner of soup made from carrots, chicken, rice, lemon and vinegar, followed by thin rolled pancakes filled with ground meat, topped with sour cream and a bright red relish made from sweet peppers. On the way to our rooms the hotel proprietor intercepted us. An envelope had been left at the desk. Our names were inscribed on it in the same handwriting and same red ink as the mysterious notes. It contained two tickets for Zorka's Magical Marionette Show.

Chapter VIII

Zorka's Magical Marionette Show

It was the day of the performance. Evening drew in. We set off on foot for Zorka's Magical Marionette Show, entering an artisan quarter of wagon-makers, carpenters, rope-makers, tailors and coppersmiths. Women wore their hair plaited, woven with flowers and other adornments, tied back with long oval hair-pins. The glass bead necklaces, metal belts, bracelets and blouses decorated with silk tassels reminded me of Bulgaria. A gunsmith sat in front of his store filling cartridges, a commodity clearly in great demand.

We arrived at a patch of open ground on which a large tent had been erected. At the entrance, a man with a dancing bear and an assistant with a tambourine were drumming up custom for the marionette show. The tambourine was in competition with an opportunistic little street orchestra of viola, two drums, a flute and a triangle. A girl hardly more than twelve years of age inspected our tickets. She showed us to seats reserved in our name. On a stage backdrop, large snakes rose from the ground and swept across fields. Among the serpents a group of crudely-painted gravity-defying peasants danced the rondo in quick time.

A Gipsy musical ensemble in velveteen coats with glittering buckles on their clogs sat at one side of the stage, scraping at fiddles. Puppeteers and seamstresses lit by oil-lamps lifted marionettes from a great carved chest painted pea-green and picked out with scarlet and gold. The dolls were about two feet tall, made from hand-carved poplar. Two or three of the female marionettes wore white tulle dresses over pink silk slips, hair arranged *à la grecque*. Other girl-marionettes lay crumpled in a small heap, some with wide kilted skirts and velvet or satin aprons embroidered with posies of red roses and pansies. The male marionettes were dressed as village dandies in frilled white shirts, velvet waistcoats and high boots, with a bright flower behind an ear. A girl reached deep into the chest and pulled out a witch marionette with bandaged feet and a black cat gripping hard to her shoulder.

With a mouthful of pins, a seamstress worked rapidly to turn up the hem of a fierce-looking marionette. A large, bristly handlebar moustache dangled loosely to its chin. A shako on his head showed a military background. Fifteen minutes later, the Gipsy musicians jumped to their feet and struck up in earnest, singing in loud, forced voices. The audience hushed. The marionettes sprang into life as palmists, sorcerers, or fortune tellers turning over decks of Tarot cards. They joined hands and began to dance a *kolo*, turning in a ring, hands on each other's shoulders and waists, first a few steps to the right, then a few steps to the left, or backwards and forwards.

Cameo scenes came and went until a drum roll indicated we were at the final Act. Slowly, to joyous calls from the marionettes, a wooden crib descended from the dark of the roof. The cot tilted and swayed like a lifeboat lowered in a storm. The marionettes crowded around it, welcoming a new baby into the world. Their hand movements and excited exclamations proclaimed their delight. The proud terracotta mother hovered over the troupe, looking down. On one foot she wore an ugly orthopaedic shoe. A marionette broke an egg for luck over the face of the new-born infant. Other marionettes swung into a wild dance, with nimble, high-stepping footwork as though to give zest to the new soul. The swirling *kolo* reached a frenzy.

A crash of thunder rattled the small auditorium. The wild dancing came to an abrupt halt. A disquieting barefoot human hurled herself swooping and twirling into the throng of marionettes. Dark hair fell in an avalanche of curls on the left eye, obscuring her face. A paste made from talc and tamarind seeds applied to the face, hands and feet gave a lustrous ivory glow to her skin. A black pearl drooped heavily from one ear, a pink pearl from the other, giving an odd and bewildering witchery. As though the lid had been lifted off a beehive, a buzz rose from the audience. In awed whispers, the name 'Zorka' seeped around the auditorium.

With an air of menacing command, Zorka ordered the marionettes to turn back and look again into the cot. One by one they obeyed. They went strangely silent as they stared down more intently at the new-born infant. A female marionette called out, beseeching someone in the outer darkness to approach. A midwife puppet appeared and examined the infant. With a high-pitched cry of anguish she turned to face the audience, her hands clasped in prayer. The music switched tempo from joyous to menacing. The musicians broke into a shrill falsetto in an attempt to frighten off the evil eye, a wild, inhuman sound. The marionettes crowded around the cot, beseeching the spirits to reverse the damage to the newborn's brain. The agonised mother cried out, realising something terrible was about to happen.

The sturdy moustachioed marionette of military aspect and middle years made his entry. One arm was unnaturally enlarged, like the giant claw of the Fiddler Crab. A prolonged scream of horror and anguish burst from the other marionettes, sick with

111

fear as the threat to the new-born infant became clear. Zorka struggled desperately to hold him back. They lurched back and forth across the stage and down into the audience. The powerful wooden arm of the military marionette sent Zorka crashing to the ground. He turned and stretched his merciless hands down into the cot to throttle the child. He lifted up the lifeless body. The auditorium went black. The air was filled with the sound of a hundred voices screaming, marionettes and audience alike.

Absurdly, hypnotically, a stone started to trundle out over the audience, lit up from behind the stage by a single beam no larger than a coin. The stone halted above where Holmes and I were seated, rocking gently on the wires. My comrade reached up and took hold of it. Scratched on it were the words *Ukleta kuća*.

Outside the tent, relieved to be away from the horror of the infanticide, I asked, 'Holmes, what on Earth could all this mean?'

Holmes replied grimly, 'The marionettes have presented us with a conundrum. If that was Rózsika's child mentioned by Besso, she was born an imbecile and murdered. One thing is certain, we are no longer searching for a living being. We seek a corpse. The question is, why are we to take an interest in the fate of Rózsika's child? What has that to do with Einstein?'

I added, 'And what are we to make of the words '*Ukleta kuća*'?'

'I must encourage you to learn German,' Holmes replied. 'With just Pashto and Hindi at your command you are at a considerable disadvantage in this matter.'

Holmes's command of the language was legendary, and not employed solely to read great works of science in their original tongue. To my knowledge he had quoted Goethe in the original three times. He had even conquered the *Fraktur* type and the confusing majuscule of *eszett*.

'How would speaking German help?' I asked. 'Surely the words *Ukleta kuća* are in the local language?'

'You miss the point, Watson. The significance for our quest is the fact the message was scratched into a stone. The German for a stone is *Ein Stein*. Remember the nickname for Mileva's son – *Steinli*, Little Stone?'

I retired early. I was on the point of getting into bed when a tap at the door produced my comrade.

'Watson, I was just passing by and saw your light on. I am sorry to trouble you, but I have a further question concerning the Café Bollwerk. Do you recall Mileva's words when we met there – the way she described her infant boy?'

'Only that he's called Hans Albert,' I replied. 'Is there something curious about that? Surely Hans and Albert are perfectly standard German names?'

'Not the names, Watson, but how she went on to describe him,' Holmes replied.

I reached across for my note-book. As I expected, I had not recorded such an inconsequential matter. I begged, 'Given you appear to feel the matter is of staggering importance, Holmes, would you be good enough to refresh my memory – and then let me get a night's sleep?'

'I shall, my dear friend, certainly. I believe Mileva's exact words were "He's our first son".'

'Those were certainly her words. What's so unusual about that?'

'Her "first son",' Holmes repeated. 'By which she means what?'

113

'Simply that Hans Albert was the first of several sons they plan to have,' I replied.

'You may be right, Watson,' my comrade replied thoughtfully. 'Nevertheless I shall tuck it away and see whether it withers at the vine or bursts into glorious life further down the track. It's time to follow the clue we were given in the second note. To-morrow we go to Titel.'

As he turned away he said, 'Zorka is making allegations against Miloš Marić based on what knowledge? If the events portrayed by the marionettes are true, how do you suppose she got to know about them? Only the closest members of the Marić family would have been party to a matter as terrible as this.'

Chapter IX

We Discover the *Ukleta kuća*

In the morning we set off for Titel, passing the location of the marionette show. The tent had been struck. Now just a few sheep awaiting slaughter grazed the patch of ground. The long poles of the tarantass carriage reduced the jolting of long-distance travel. We spent the journey resting on straw within the basket, safe from the ever-present mud and manure flung up by the horses' hooves.

Titel was a scattered collection of houses thirty miles from Novi-Sad, more hamlet than village. The larger houses were of brick, stuccoed and painted a dusty pink. They sat in their own vegetable and flower gardens. Most had clumps of fan-shaped yellow irises sacred to Basilicum, god of thunder and lightning, highest of the Slavic pantheon. Vendors stood at every street corner, their three-legged tables piled up with circular bread with sesame seeds known by the local name *đevrek*. The tarantass dropped us off at the Hotel Kondor. It was hardly more than a coaching inn. A saloon pistol and rook rifle dangled from pegs on the wall. The Proprietor was a short man with a bold hooked nose and gold-rimmed spectacles. He spoke English with fluent inaccuracy. A stuffed macaw perched behind him in a glass case. We signed our nationality and date of arrival into his book.

'My esteemed guests, I see you are from the land of the blackbird and robin,' our host began.

'I have many visitors who follow that fine English tradition of bird-surveying. You may already know our beloved forests and meadowlands and cliffs are renowned for their variety of species (he paused to point behind him at the macaw), not least the Spotted Eagle. With the advent of summer, you will find the squacco heron, the black stork, the eagle owl, the hoopoe, the lesser grey shrike. Even as we speak the fieldfare loses its winter grey. What else. Ah, yes, all sorts of warblers, the great reed, barred, and the olive-tree warbler.'

I asked to see our rooms. They were comfortably furnished with rattan chairs and water-colour paintings of English cathedrals, the jalousies drawn against the heat of the outside world. We returned with our host to the front desk. I said we had a question to ask him. He beamed. He welcomed any question we might wish to put to him. About the pied wheateater perhaps? I showed him the inscription on the stone and asked the translation of *Ukleta kuća*. The smile disappeared. He took a sharp step backward, startled and disturbed.

'*Ukleta kuća,*' he repeated.

Why would we want to know about that?

'About what?' I asked.

He came from behind the desk and beckoned us to join him by the armchairs. 'You do not know what *Ukleta kuća* means?'

'Not the slightest idea,' I agreed.

His voice dropped.

'In your language it means haunted hearth, by which we mean haunted house. Once upon a time it was a fine house. Now it's fallen down. No-one goes anywhere near it.'

His voice dropped further, obliging us to lean forward until our three heads nearly touched.

'I shall tell you a story,' he whispered. 'Twenty-eight years ago a stranger came to this village.'

He pointed sideways. 'From that direction. North. They said he was once a man of importance in Vukovar. A *Landsschef.* He had been an Army officer. No-one knew where his money came from and nobody asked. He purchased two hundred *hectares* of land. He brought in a flock of more than fifty sheep and put them into a cleared field. It's our custom to use such animals to find the healthiest spot to build a house. Sheep go to the driest part of the field to spend the night. Where the flock lay down he built a *Zidana*, a large house with embellished eaves and a cupola containing a brass bell. He called the house *Kula* which means tower in your language. He brought a priest from Kać, the region of his birth, to bless his new home with holy water.'

Holmes asked, 'Do you recall the name of the family?'

'Marić,' came the response. 'Miloš Marić. He was a man who stayed aloof. He had two daughters. In our region a man who has only daughters will tell you he is childless. Miloš Marić was double-cursed – both daughters were born with one leg shorter than the other. Around here the youngest was known as *mirna ludakinja* which means the quiet loony. Everyone was afraid of her. Rumours circulated around the village. A child was born – they said the *mirna ludakinja* was the mother. The very next day after the birth the priest came to bless the baby. That was unusual. It's our custom not to bless a child until 40 days after the birth.'

He leaned forward even more conspiratorially. 'Around two years later – it was a September - something terrible must have taken place. The priest was summoned back from Kać. Miloš Marić was seen creeping into the church of the Virgin Mary's

Ascension at an unusual hour. Shortly afterwards, he endowed the church with a new bell. It was so big it took a team of six oxen to bring it from the railway depôt to the campanile.'

All three of us had begun to straighten up. The proprietor bent forward again. Once more our heads went down with his. 'One night the house caught fire. Everyone in the village rushed over to help put out the flames. A wagon piled up with the Marić family's belongings was ready to depart. The servant whispered the family were convinced an evil spirit had taken up residence. The spirit warned the family never to leave, but after the servant saw a bad omen – a snake falling from a plum tree – Miloš Marić made up his mind the family should abandon the house. They chose a time when the spirit might be asleep. No sooner had they loaded their possessions on the wagon to leave than the flames erupted. The family fled the minute we arrived without making any effort to save the house. Some weeks later, a villager walking close-by late at night felt a drop in temperature. He heard distorted voices and the sound of a woman weeping. He saw ghostly emanations on the back porch, crowded around a dreadful object at their feet. The spirits turned to stare at the villager. Before he could run away the ghosts vanished.'

The hotel proprietor assured us he didn't believe in spirits from the Other World. He had spent many years in England, in Manchester, as manager of the famous Ascott Hotel, did we know it? But here in Serbia, the villagers – they believe *Kula* is haunted by a *rusalka*. Not even stray dogs go near the house.

'What does *rusalka* mean?' I asked. I had heard the children whispering the word at Zorka's Magical Marionette performance.

'A *rusalka* is an unquiet dead being, mostly female,' came the reply. 'Women and girls who die violently and before their time. Young women who commit suicide because they have been jilted by their lovers, or unbaptised children, often those born out of wedlock. They must live out their designated time on Earth as disturbed spirits. As to your visiting the ruins...'

He tried to dissuade us. What possible reason could we have for visiting a haunted house? Didn't we understand what we were getting ourselves into? This is not your country, he reminded us. This is the Balkans. To-day was the seventh day after the spring new moon, a time the spirits of the unredeemed attempt a return. Why choose tonight of all nights? Evil abounded. Besides he was certain no-one would take us there. He would offer, but unfortunately he had commitments here at the hotel.

Faced with our obduracy he gave up. He warned us to keep our destination secret or the villagers might mistake us for necromancers. We could stir up trouble for ourselves, and for him. The locals would accuse us of summoning up spirits of the undead or raising the dead for the purpose of divination. He had one last piece of advice. If we insisted on pursuing this reckless plan we must disguise our intent. He would instruct a cabby to take us to the Church of Virgin Mary's Ascension, a quarter-hour walk from the haunted house. The driver would retrieve us from the church after a passage of two hours. We should safeguard ourselves in the sight of Heaven and the villagers by lighting candles in front of the painting of the Black Madonna. His hand trembled as he handed us three beeswax candles, one for each of us and one for him. Before we set off, would we please leave instructions where to send our luggage (and how our bill should be paid) if the worst came to the worst?

The cab was an ugly but utilitarian glass-fronted four-wheeler owned by the proprietor's cousin. We banged from side to side as the horses plunged at a furious pace over the cobblestones and on through the narrow street of furriers towards the isolated Church of Virgin Mary's Ascension. Outside the village we slowed over an unmetalled track, its surface deeply rutted by the passage of bullock-carts. Pigeons overtook us at speed, intent on getting to water before dark. A boy and a girl, possibly siblings, sat begging at the church entrance. Both urchins had leather peasant sandals, fashioned from rough pieces of hide. The boy wore baggy brown breeches and a high-buttoned shirt homespun from flax and wool. The girl was about nine years old, with the self-possession of an adult. She was brown as a berry, dressed in a dirty old scarlet frock which had shed its fastenings. In broken German she said, 'I am *ciganka*. You are *gorgiki*. Where do you come from?'

'England,' Holmes told her. She had never heard of our native land.

Holmes handed each of them a *thaler*. Two pairs of eyes opened wide in wonderment. I asked the young Gipsies to confirm the direction of the *Ukleta kuća*. On hearing the words they pointed and fled. We lit the three candles at the shrine of the Black Madonna and left the church. In the fast-diminishing light we saw the outline of our destination. An overgrown path took us from the church towards the dilapidated house. The roof had caved in. Timbered, almost a perfect square, the *Kula* was constructed of fired bricks packed between wooden uprights and whitewashed. The lopsided shape and air of dereliction paid tribute to the harshness of the Balkan winter.

We entered the front garden through an ornate filigreed wrought-iron railing. The fact that such a costly artefact was still *in situ* bore silent witness to the terror the ruin inspired. Withered violas and sunflowers drooped from disintegrating trellises around the porch, the seeds long since harvested by birds over winter. Tufts of dead weeds poked up through outdoor stone steps leading to the ruined second level.

At ten feet from the door a demonic sound swept over us, a harsh and disembodied female voice which might have come rushing up from the soil beneath us or sweeping towards us from some distant cavern. I understood the words to say 'Halt there, do not come nearer' but to this day I cannot swear in which language the words were spoken. My heart palpitated dangerously. Holmes pulled me back.

'Stay still, Watson,' came the low reply. 'She is here. We've been brought to a place of augury.'

Holmes turned back to the ruin. 'Have you brought us here because you wish us harm?' he called out.

A small object flew out and fell before us. It was a dried bean, painted green. I picked it up and passed it to my companion.

'What do you make of this, Holmes?' I whispered.

'This is like the Oracle at Delphi,' he replied loudly. 'It is up to us to ask questions. They must be put to her in ways which can be answered by one or other of these coloured beans. If I'm right a red bean means yes, the green bean means no.'

'Isn't that so?' he called out. A red bean dropped at my feet.

Holmes resumed his questions. Had she written the two notes shown to us by Professor Sobel? Red. Was it her intention to prevent Einstein gaining employment at the University? Green. Was the answer to why she had brought us to Serbia close to us now? Red.

We heard the sound of a carriage departing. Holmes lit a match and pushed open the dilapidated door. Scattered around the dust-ridden room were abandoned crocks, jugs, and a plethora of measuring containers and ladles. At the far side stood a charred screen decorated with icons. With a swift movement Holmes pushed it aside. A second burning match illuminated brass incense-burners, black with fire and age. From every hook and beam hung the marionettes from Zorka's Magical Marionette Theatre, every eye upon us. At head height in front of us dangled the moustachioed military marionette. Close-set, unrepentant eyes stared at us, the same eyes which had turned to glare directly upon us after he had murdered the child. The forefinger of his huge outstretched arm pointed onward.

We followed the direction indicated by the spectral figure and came to a small flight of steps leading out to the overgrown back-garden. A spade stood upright in the ground. A piece of cloth was draped over the handle. It was the blanket from the child's crib.

My companion gestured towards the lowest step. 'You have your orders, Watson. Dig there.'

Two minutes passed. We stood looking down into the shallow excavation. Barely five inches below the surface a pair of empty eye sockets stared up at us. I brushed the rest of the soil from the bones. The energetic activity of the topsoil had corroded the flesh of a child between eighteen months and two years of age.

The skeleton had the appearance of being placed hurriedly in the resting-place. I pulled out my old Army compass. The tiny corpse lay along an uneven north-east axis.

'She wasn't given a Christian burial,' I remarked, 'or she would lie on an east-west axis. They were clearly in a hurry. According to our hotel proprietor she may be a *rusalka* by now.'

'You say 'she', Watson?'

'I think we can say it's female,' I affirmed. 'At birth the skeletal maturation as a whole is more advanced in girls, while compared to a boy's these arm and leg bones are shorter.'

The line of bones lay loosely together, held by the tattered linen remnants of her frock. The agony of the contorted limbs struck me with a spasm of pain. My eyes blurred with tears. Wisps of dark hair still sprouted from the scalp, straggling down into the eye sockets. Tiny gold studs lay where the ear-lobes had been. I patted the hair into place. The sad assembly could hardly have filled our tin *vasculum*. After a minute I rose to my feet.

'I can confirm the child's fate, Holmes. It was exactly as acted out by the puppeteers.'

My voice trembled. I pointed to a horseshoe-shaped bone between the chin and the thyroid cartilage. 'Look at the lingual bone.'

'What about it?' Holmes demanded, kneeling down.

'It's fractured. She was throttled by someone using considerable force. They wanted it over with quickly.'

As though he were interrogating the bones Holmes said, 'If this is Rózsika's child... what does it all mean? Why have we have been brought to this grave? The author of those notes is telling us something, Watson, yet it is in no way clear to me what is wanted of us.'

He pushed himself up. 'Replace the soil, my friend. We must talk to someone who can interpret what's going on, what this all means. It's time to take up Mycroft's suggestion. To-morrow we go to meet Miss Edith Durham.'

Chapter X

We Meet Edith Durham

Another tarantass took us to the Vaskrsenja Hristova Monastery. A young monk conducted us in silence to the Archimandrite, a tall man in the long black robes and high cap of the Orthodox ecclesiasts. He spoke in the oddest broken French.

'From England,' he repeated several times, incredulously. 'Like Madame Durham, all the way from England to see Serbia. *Quelle voyage! Veritablement des heros!*' He assured us we were welcome, 'for we are Christians, and is not hospitality one of the first of the Christian virtues?'

The mention of Edith Durham set us on the trail to meet her. She was visible from some way off, seated at an artist's easel a short distance from the river bank, dressed as the New Woman *in fiocchi* – shirtwaist, tall stiff collar, necktie, and heavy serge skirt. The hair was cropped boyishly, the face neither plain nor pretty. I thought, so this is the intrepid woman who wanders through the Balkans among Albanians, Serbs, Croats, Bosnians, Slovaks and a dozen other tribes and religions. Her observations and conclusions formed from scouring the Peninsular would be finding their way back to the new Foreign Secretary Sir Edward Grey.

'So you are Mycroft's famous brother,' she said, inspecting Holmes as intently as she had been staring at the dead snake-eyed skink she was in the midst of painting.

'Wasn't spying a rather dangerous occupation, here in the Cockpit of Europe?' I asked. Shortly after Holmes and I were last in the Balkans an American missionary by the name of Miss Stone was kidnapped and held to ransom on the Bulgarian border. Negotiations with the bandits were bungled and she was murdered. Miss Durham appeared undaunted.

'I tell everyone I am like the Brothers Grimm, collecting folk tales and local superstitions,' she replied. 'For example, Dr. Watson, do you know the local cure for epilepsy? As a medical man you might find it useful.'

'I don't know, I'm afraid,' I replied.

'If you see a snake swallowing a frog, you must throw a black handkerchief over it. This gives the snake such a fright it disgorges the frog. The handkerchief can then be thrown over the head of anyone suffering an epileptic fit. The sufferer will immediately disgorge the disease.'

'What is the reason you are touring Serbia at this time?' Holmes enquired.

'The Pig War, of course,' Miss Durham replied.

I struggled to keep a straight face. 'The Pig War!' I exclaimed.

'There are rumours of an impending pig war between the Habsburg Empire and the Kingdom of Serbia,' she explained.

'What exactly is a Pig War?' I asked, exploding with laughter.

'You may consider a customs' war a trivial matter, Dr. Watson,' Miss Durham chided, 'but it could lead to a general war. Pigs produced in Serbia are sold to the Austria-Hungarians who are now threatening an embargo. The pig market forms only a tiny part of the Austria-Hungarian economy, but it's of over-riding importance to the Serbs. Serbia's Liberals and Radicals are fanatically devoted to Russia. They follow a policy of irritating Vienna at every opportunity. Belgrade will break the embargo by selling her pigs via the Adriatic to France. A stratagem of this sort would seriously rile Franz Joseph and raise the temperature enormously.'

'Why should that be of any special concern to England?' I asked, perplexed.

'Destabilisation in this region could have the severest consequences for the whole of Europe.'

The exchange was followed by an awkward silence. The Tisza River was huge, fast and muddy. We stared at a dead sheep among the flotsam surging past. Miss Durham broke the silence,

'Now, tell me how I can be helpful'

I launched into a detailed account, how we had been commissioned by Berne University to investigate the background of a potential member of the faculty by the name of Albert Einstein. We had not met the young man but we had met his Serb wife, Mileva and their baby son, Hans Albert. I told her Mileva's younger sister, Rózsika had hung back, too shy to approach us. I showed the two notes and explained how Holmes had deduced "Titel" was a small town in Serbia, but we had drawn a complete blank on "Lieserl". We had scoured official records in Novi-Sad with no results. I mentioned the arrival of tickets for Zorka's Magical Marionette Show and its dramatic plot. Finally, I handed Miss Durham the inscribed stone which had led us to the discovery of the tiny skeleton at a haunted house in Titel.

She looked up from the painting. 'And now?' she asked.

'We have no idea how to proceed,' I replied.

'You say the skeleton was that of a girl of perhaps twenty months of age?'

'Within two or three months either way, yes.'

'And she was choked to death?'

'Yes.'

'And the burial was, to say the least, hastily done?'

I nodded.

Miss Durham went on, 'It's not unknown in this part of the world for a palsied baby to be put to death.' She was silent for several minutes. Then she asked, 'Are you at all *au fait* with the law here – based as it is on Roman law?' she asked.

We admitted we had little or no familiarity with local laws.

'Then I shall tell you the laws of Serbia. If the mother kills a child when it is less than twelve months old, the court will rule she has done so while her equilibrium remained disturbed from giving birth. If the child is killed *after* the age of twelve months, by the mother or anyone else, it's deemed murder. The penalty is death. In Belgrade the culprit would be taken to a place unfrequented by the public and shot. In the towns and villages like Novi-Sad or Titel the authorities are less respectful. The shooting would take place in public.'

Miss Durham looked at me with a slight lift of her eyebrows. 'Are you now quite as surprised to find you can discover no trace of documents or anybody who will talk?'

She dipped the paint brush into a blob of suitably reptilian green paint. 'Dr. Watson, you have, no doubt, described the sequence of events correctly, but there is one point which you have failed to include.'

I was startled at her remonstrance. 'I am sure I, I...' I stammered.

'I heard you met someone connected to the Marić family.'

'Ah that, yes,' I confessed. 'Jelena. I did leave her out – but for good reason.'

'Which is...?' came the query.

'That despite crossing her palm with gold, we learnt nothing.' I shrugged ruefully. 'Unless, Miss Durham, it's of interest to anyone what small gifts Mileva made to Einstein.'

She withdrew the brush sharply from the canvas. 'Why should the woman give you that particular information?'

'Perhaps to avoid telling us anything of importance,' I hazarded.

'And these gifts Mileva made to Einstein?' Miss Durham asked.

'Shirts. She told us Mileva gave Einstein shirts. She burst into song, in fact.'

'And gave you the English translation?'

I nodded. Miss Durham stared from one to other of us. She bent down and put the snake-eyed skink into a small box out of the warm sun.

'Were the words, *"In Banok and Bjelopavlice. She called to everyone. To everyone she gave a shirt"*?'

'Why yes,' I replied.

'And it was definitely Mileva she referred to? Mileva gave Einstein the shirts? You are certain of that?'

'Without any doubt.' I pointed at Holmes. 'My good friend here will tell you that I take assiduous notes.'

Her face took on a curious expression. The paint brush went back into the jar. 'And you have no idea what this particular gift means?'

Without waiting for my reply she went on, 'I can tell you. To say a woman gave a man a shirt means she had intimate relations with him. Out of wedlock. We would call her a woman of loose morals, a 'clergyman's daughter'.'

She retrieved the skink and paint brush and turned back to the canvas. 'Gentlemen, I want to finish this before the light changes.'

As we left, Miss Durham called out, 'Mr. Holmes, may I ask you two favours in return for any help I have managed to provide? The George Edalji case. I have been following it. When you get back to London, could you look into the matter? The man has been accused of writing menacing letters and slashing ponies. His father was a Parsi. I believe him to be completely innocent. And secondly, before you return to Berne, I would like you to take a small gift from me to a Father Florus at a small church not far from here, Our Lady Among the Rocks.'

She reached into a capacious bag and brought out a tin of sausages and another of pears. She dipped back into the bag. Out came a small book of Verlaine's poetry.

'And this, too. By special request of the Father,' she added.

I returned to take possession of the slim volume and tins. 'Is the church far?' I enquired dubiously.

'Think of Bunyan,' she replied ominously. '"When I came to the foot of the hill called Difficulty, I met with a very aged man, who asked me what I was, and whither bound. I told him that I am a pilgrim, going to the Celestial City".' She added, 'You will discover how poor the roadways are here. In their world, after all, a road that will serve a cart will serve the rapacious Turk and his artillery.'

With a farewell wave she called out, 'Gentlemen, I wish you *in bocca al lupo!* – the best of luck. You swim in dangerous waters. The moment you fit the pieces together, I suggest you waste no time in quitting the Balkans. What you might discover will leave you vulnerable to revenge. Desperate to avoid family disgrace, Miloš Marić will offer a reward to any passing *hajduci* to take care of you. You are out of danger only while he believes you have discovered nothing.'

She added, without a trace of a smile, 'though if the worst happens, you may rely on me to publish your obituaries in *The Times*.'

Unperturbed, my comrade responded, 'In which eventuality, Miss Durham, it would be good of you to deliver my head to a James Mortimer, House-surgeon.'

'Address?'

'The Charing Cross Hospital. During the Baskerville affair he took a cast of my head and made me promise to give him the genuine article in the course of time.'

At this we thanked her for her help and picked up our fishing tackle. I was eager to commence. Chub, carp and barbell in the Tisza were said to match a trout for speed and surpass it for power.

We were some yards away when she called after us a second time: 'Mr. Holmes, the name of the puppet show, tell me again?'

I replied in Holmes's stead. 'Zorka's Magical Marionette Show.'

'And Einstein's sister-in-law – her first name?'

'Rózsika.'

On the breeze Miss Durham's words came to us. 'That would be her full Christian name. Down here her family and friends would use the popular term of endearment for Rózsika.'

'What would that be?' I called back.

'Zorka.'

***

Out of earshot of this most remarkable woman I grasped Holmes's elbow.

'Holmes,' I exclaimed, 'the marionette show – '

'Rózsika and Zorka. One and the same.'

I cast my mind back to the dark, silent creature observing us from afar at the Café Bollwerk.

'Therefore the marionette play… ' I began.

'Staged by Mileva's sister.'

'So it must have been Rózsika at the haunted house!'

'Without doubt, one and the same. I too can make no sense of it, Watson. Why would Rózsika-cum-Zorka want us to know how her infant daughter died? What does it matter? Why would she send those notes to the Rector? I ask again, what could it possibly have to do with Einstein?'

We had hardly settled ourselves at the river when with a loud cry Holmes struck himself across the forehead.

'Of course - of *course*, Watson! You and I are the most absolute fools in Europe! What blunderers we have been!'

'Steady, Holmes,' I protested. 'Perhaps you could enlighten me as to…'

'The marionette, my dear fellow, the marionette! The mother. The one hovering above the cradle!'

'What about her?'

'The orthopaedic shoe. Which foot was it on, the right or the left?'

'The left.'

'Precisely! Every detail of the plot was exact, right down to the displacement of which hip. Answer me this,' Holmes commanded, 'when you observed Rózsika at the Café Bollwerk, she rested on her deformed foot, is it not so?'

'As would one with such an affliction,' I affirmed.

'Which foot? Think hard, my friend! Remember, she was facing us.'

'The right foot, Holmes. Definitely her right foot.'

'You are certain? It is of the utmost importance.'

'No doubt whatsoever, my dear fellow. I am a medical man. I took particular note because this affliction strikes mostly at the other hip.'

'So as the puppet wore the shoe on her *left* foot, Watson – ?'

I stared at my companion in the uttermost astonishment. I stammered, 'The puppeteer was telling us the infant was not Rózsika's child after all. She was … '

'Mileva's. That is precisely what the puppeteer was telling us. At the time I thought the shoe had been placed on the left foot at random but it was not so.'

'And therefore the father is – '

'Who else but the one to whom Mileva gave shirts.'

'Einstein!' I cried out. 'Lieserl was Einstein's daughter!'

***

Back in the Vaskrsenja Hristova Monastery, Holmes spoke.

'Once more I need you to remind me. What was it Besso said about Mileva when we met at the Bollwerk Café, something about a dramatic change? You were scribbling away at the time. The exact words, please.'

I pulled out my note-book and flicked back through the pages.

'Besso said, "Quite suddenly her mood changed - I can't explain it any other way than that she stopped smiling. One day she was a lively person, the next she was visibly distraught". He went on to say, "Something must have happened between Mileva and Albert".'

'And when did Besso say that change occurred?' asked Holmes.

'Around September 1903.'

'The skeleton, Watson. When do you estimate the little girl was placed in the ground?'

'About that very time – within a few weeks either way,' I replied.

'The military puppet represented Mileva's father. He was once a soldier. The moment Mileva heard of her child's death she knew.'

'She knew what?'

'That it was her father and only *he* could have carried out Lieserl's murder with Einstein's agreement.'

'Holmes,' I said, brimming with anger, 'we must set off immediately. We must reveal this at once to the Rector and Professor Sobel. For Einstein to condone, perhaps incite, the killing of his baby girl, even one with a badly-damaged brain – the wretch deserves whatever punishment he's due.'

Chapter XI

We Meet Father Florus

The monks were up and about by the time I went for breakfast in the simple refectory. Despite my keenness to return to Berne there was an undertaking to fulfil. We had to deliver Miss Durham's gifts to Father Florus at the Church of Our Lady Among the Rocks. Archimandrite Nikanor greeted me. I explained we were postponing our fishing in favour of a visit to Father Florus. A *kavass*, a Serbian guide, was summoned to escort us. The Archimandrite led us though a little stone-paved room hung with portraits of the Czar and Czaritsa of Russia out to the start of a well-marked footpath among wild pomegranates. Our *kavass* led off, a heavy lantern swinging from his hand in case darkness overtook us on our return.

Away from the monastery any semblance of a road capable of supporting a cart ended abruptly. All around was wild, untouched rock, the scent of cistus and thyme on the hill-sides. Shrub oak jutted up among outcrops. Occasional abrupt descents left us slithering and sliding down the sides of stony ravines. Now and then a small flock of sheep pressed past us, hurrying to fresh pastures, driven by little girls with eyebrows blackened, their hair dyed a red as fierce as the bright crimson of the local rams.

Our pace slowed as the altitude increased. Now and then a palisaded village came into view. On patches given over to vegetables, bent figures pushed potatoes, turnips, onions and garlic into the well-prepared soil. At one point we stopped to resupply our water from an artesian well sited by a moving fringe of dogs and crude lean-to toilets. Our *kavass* told us that in times of danger the villagers took refuge in the most inaccessible gorges.

From above us came the first low growl of a storm. 'Thunder,' I called ahead to Holmes's back.

'Evidently,' he replied over his shoulder.

To take my attention off my aching legs, my mind returned to fishing. I thought about the time when, aged twelve, I went for my first night-fishing expedition. I made a great deal of noise stumbling around and fell down, wrenching a shoulder, and never caught a thing.

Mycroft had sent us the most wonderful fishing tackle. During the short time on the Tisza, the Hardy Perfect reel and Mr. W. Senior's Red Spinners had proved themselves. I needed more time to try out the favourite chub-fly of the late Mr. Francis, a complicated matter of grilse size, silver tinsel, and a tail of white kid glove or wash leather. Cheered by these happy reflections, I returned to the present. Holmes had taken the lead, maintaining a relentless pace up the ever-steepening slope. We passed through the ruins of an ancient forum. Green acanthus flourished between the stony leaves of fallen Corinthian capitals. It was now noon. Our guide pointed to a second stony track round the hillside. A ridge of rocks ended in a sheer cliff overlooking a stone-strewn slope.

'You are there,' he said. 'Pass between those,' he continued, pointing at two immense boulders. 'You will find the Father beyond them.'

We squeezed between the boulders and spied a tall figure in the tattered black cassock of a priest. He was aged between thirty-five and forty. Father Florus stepped forward to welcome us.

'Miss Durham sent word you would be coming. I watched you all the way across the plain in case you had an encounter with the *Veele*. In South-Slavic mythology the *Veele* are fairy-like spirits.'

He recounted how the *Veele* live in the wilderness and sometimes in the clouds, spirits of women who had been frivolous in their lifetimes and now float between here and the afterlife. They appear as swans, snakes, horses, falcons or wolves, 'but usually as beautiful maidens, naked or dressed in white with long flowing hair'. The priest sighed.

'The voices of the *Veele* are beautiful. One who hears them loses all thoughts of food, drink or sleep. However,' he continued, smiling, 'despite their feminine charms the *Veele* are fierce warriors. The earth is said to shake when they do battle.'

I handed Father Florus a carp sent with the Archimandrite's regards, followed by the gifts from Edith Durham. He picked up the book of Verlaine's poems and quoted from it: '*Voici des fruits, des fleurs, des feuilles et des branches*'.

He looked at me. 'One needs little in this life,' he said. 'We have so short a time here.'

Father Florus turned towards his tiny domain, a bare stone wall standing against the hillside with a wooden cross at the top, and a two-roomed cottage with a patch of cultivated ground close by. With a further heavy rumble of thunder the heavens opened. The priest pointed at an opening in the mountain. 'We can find shelter over there. In my little church,' he said, leading the way.

The cave entrance was devoid of any attempt at architecture. Not a capital, pilaster, pediment, moulding, cornice, or porch broke the baldness. Tiny tawdry objects had been pushed into cracks in the rock. We entered a long narrow cavern, water-worn, with traces of stalactite deposit on the rough walls. Two settles served for pews for the scanty congregation. Torches burned brightly, lighting up a picture of Our Lady, their sap releasing an acrid but pleasant odour. A smaller cave opened on either side, making a ready-made nave and transept.

The Father said, 'The people say this church was built by the Hand of God. His hands in the wilderness. *Si non è vero, è ben trovato* – even if it's not true it makes a good story. Is it not in the form of a cross?'

He motioned towards a bier covered with a black and gold cloth, and an illustration of the dead Christ. 'Here, you see, I have made the Holy Sepulchre.'

The walls at the chancel end were covered with saints and angels, quaint and stiff, their archaic Byzantine forms in perfect keeping with the rough surroundings. Father Florus crossed himself, his chrysoprase ring catching the torch-light.

'When I pray all alone in the silence, then holy things come to me, pictures, *vous savez*. I paint them here upon the wall.'

His otherwise serious face broke into a soft and pleasant expression. 'My poor attempts at painting give pleasure to my people, and they understand. These are the last I have made. There is no paint left.'

'Were you always here?' my comrade enquired politely.

'No. Once upon a time I was elsewhere.'

'Novi-Sad?' Holmes asked.

The priest shook his head.

'No. Not Novi-Sad. Over there. Kać.'

He placed his hands on a silver bowl and an etched crystal goblet of water placed by the silver cross. 'We are expecting a Christening ceremony here to-morrow,' he said.

'I've heard that in Serbia an infant receives the blessing forty days after the birth. Is that correct?' Holmes asked.

The Father replied, 'Yes, after forty days, unless the baby is sickly and not expected to live.'

My comrade asked what information the church required on the forms to register the birth of a child.

'Date and place of birth,' came the reply. 'Date and place of the christening. Parents' names and ages. Name of the priest and godparents. Whether the child was a twin. The child's placement in relation to any siblings – first, second and so on. And whether defective.'

He crossed himself. His hands touched together briefly as though making a prayer. 'Or illegitimate. Most births in my region are.'

'Now,' he proclaimed, 'we eat.'

We followed him from the cool of the cave. The hot touch of the outside air on our faces warned of a stifling heat to come. Around us the ground crepitated. Pointing at the cottage, hardly more than a hovel, the priest said, 'I call this my *Konacic*. It means little palace.'

Father Florus refused to countenance our departure without a meal. 'I've been expecting you, and besides, when shall I again see visitors from England?' he exclaimed.

Appreciatively we gulped down *burek*, pastries made of filo dough filled with goat's meat and cheese. The pastries were followed by stuffed cabbage, kidney beans and potatoes, grown in his well-kept vegetable patch. After a last spoonful of sesame honey and a thick prune jam, and most of the canned peaches we had carried with us, our host led us to a departure point a hundred yards down the slope towards the boulders. He pointed into the distance. 'In two or three months those hills will be carpeted with blue periwinkles. You must return at that time.'

We said our goodbyes. The tall dark figure gave us the blessing. He turned towards the little chapel. When we had walked some distance, I looked back. There was no-one to be seen, only the low whitewashed wall, the tiny cottage and the great mountain.

Our return to the monastery was a race against the dark. The rough path led us into thick mists swirling down from the mountains. I could have done with a sturdy Shan pony. Any hope of an hour's fishing on the Tisza dissipated by the minute. By the time we reached the monastery the candle in the kavass's lantern had reached the full extent of the coiled spring on which it rested.

Before Holmes and I separated for the night I asked, 'What have we learned to-day?'

'Confirmation that the infant Lieserl was born palsied,' my comrade replied.

Chapter XII

The Denouement Looms - We Return To Berne

By sun-up, Archimandrite Nikanor was dressed and bustling about. We breakfasted with the monks on carp and rudd. Before our departure we were led to the visitors' book. Our host shook hands and murmured a blessing over us. In turn we presented him with the ferruled fishing rods, lures and spinners. We commenced the long journey back to Switzerland, starting with a tarantass to Novi-Sad. The ferry transported us across the Danube for the next leg. We settled into a comfortable railway carriage. Holmes was silent, deep in the *Baedeker*. I fell into a deep reverie, mulling over our adventures of the past few weeks with their endless twists and turns and utterly improbable discoveries, the searches in large damp boxes in dim rooms, the watchful, puzzled clerks. The feeling we were forever being observed. The jolting carriages. Jelena's song. Miss Durham's explanation.

Budapest and Vienna came and went. I interrupted my companion. 'Holmes, is it possible Mileva's father carried out the killing without Einstein's knowledge? After all, he would want to free his daughter from – '

'Impossible,' Holmes broke in emphatically. 'The infant was blessed on the first day of her life, not the customary fortieth day. Einstein would have been informed. The lack of christening records, the lack of birth certificate, the complete silence. From the moment of that blessing, Miloš and he began to hatch a plan to put Lieserl out of her – and everyone else's – misery. The mystery is why they waited so long. I can only presume Mileva – and Zorka – put up a fight.'

'And what of Mileva? Did she finally consent?'

'No. It was a *fait accompli*. It would have been a terrible shock. Besso said how she lost her happy temperament around September 1903.'

I fell silent, ruminating to the chug of the steam engine. A railway attendant opened our compartment door. We would be in Zurich in ten minutes. We changed trains. We were on the last lap. The *denouement* lay only hours ahead.

In Berne, we rang the university from our hotel. Professor Sobel insisted that we take a cab to the campus immediately. He sounded beside himself with excitement. When we entered his office, he jumped to his feet, bristling with anticipation.

'My dear sirs,' he exclaimed, 'please don't seat yourselves. The Rector has asked me to bring you to him the moment you honoured our portals again. He wishes to hear the results from the horse's mouth, I think you English say. But first ,' he held up a journal, 'have you heard the wonderful, wonderful news?'

To his delight we both shook our heads.

'While you were away Albert Einstein has startled and bewitched the whole world! He has published an extraordinary paper on the electrodynamics of moving bodies in the most learned scientific journal of all, the *Annalen der Physik*. He has come up with a theory that escaped the greatest scientific brains, George FitzGerald, Koffman, Lewis, Minkowski, Planck, even Poincaré.'

The words came to me as though filtered through cotton wool.

'The theory being?' I heard my companion ask.

'L=mV²,' came the gleeful reply. 'It's a scientific earthquake.'

Generously, the Professor brought me into the conversation. 'Dr. Watson, isn't it wonderful! L=mV². Energy equals mass times the square of the speed of light. Gravity and acceleration are essentially one and the same thing. Isn't it truly remarkable?'

I stared at him uncomprehendingly. It was clear something of immense importance in physics had taken place in our short absence. Its ramifications were beyond me, except for the fact Einstein was at the heart of it. I felt unable to look into the Professor's overjoyed face. We were bringing news of a murder in which we held Einstein complicit. Failing to note my confusion the professor rushed on.

'We must change our entire view of the universe! Young Einstein proposes that the speed of light is constant. He determines the relationship between mass and energy.'

He paused, seeking a way to bring the discussion down to my level.

'If Einstein's theory is correct, a clock located at the Equator should run slower than one at either pole. If you could go into orbit around the Earth for a month, you would be one thousandth of a second younger than those of us who stayed behind. Isn't that amazing! Don't you see, gravity is no longer a force in space and time but part of the fabric of space and time itself! Put simply, due to the equivalence of mass and energy, the gravitational field acts as its own source.'

His hands clapped together in excitement. 'Gentlemen, it's a scientific earthquake,' he repeated. 'Albert Einstein has altered the principle of Conservation. I assure you, this paper will change physics forever.'

The Professor put his hands to our shoulders. 'Come, come, Mr. Holmes, Dr. Watson. Let us hurry down to the Rector's office where you can make your report in person.'

The Rector greeted us warmly.

'Professor Sobel tells me your travels took you as far afield as Serbia. Heavens above! We are happy to welcome you back to Berne safe and sound. I trust you had an interesting time?'

We were waved to a comfortable Shenzhen sofa. Our hosts seated themselves in arm-chairs facing us. The Rector beamed from ear to ear.

He continued, 'I presume Professor Sobel has given you the news? Most remarkable. *Most* remarkable. Who would ever have thought it – except our friend here and me, of course,' he laughed, tapping his colleague's shoulder. 'The implications are immense. Isaac Newton will topple off his plinth. The focal point of physics will fly away from your Cambridge University and alight here at Berne. At *our* University.'

It was clear the Rector had put to one side the scarcely-veiled anti-Semitism and aversion to the flamboyant and rebellious young Swabian.

'Now all that remains is for you to give us the results of your investigation. Have you uncovered any skeletons in his cupboard?' at which query he and the professor broke into loud, almost raucous laughter.

Holmes placed his fingers together as he always did when poised to deliver his verdict on a matter of consequence.

I braced myself. I felt sick. 'Get on with it, Holmes,' I urged him silently. 'Tell them the wretched news and let's clear out of here.'

My comrade stared in prolonged silence at the two men before us. Their bright smiles began to fade into expressions of concern and bewilderment. Finally Holmes commenced.

'As you say, Dr. Watson and I have returned from conducting a confidential enquiry in the Balkans.'

Our hosts nodded eagerly.

'We were charged by Professor Eli Sobel here with the investigation of two notes delivered anonymously to you, Sir,' he said, looking directly at the Rector.

'Yes, yes,' came a joint response.

'The first note referred to a Swabian by the name of A. Einstein and to a Lieserl. The second note simply stated "Titel".'

The two heads nodded vigorously.

'Both notes,' Holmes went on, 'were written on cartridge paper in red ink by an anonymous and disturbing hand. My interpretation of the word "Titel" combined with the type of paper and Mileva Einstein's place of birth led us to spend some weeks in the Kingdom of Serbia.'

By now I had been brought to a pitch of exasperation. '*For Heaven's sake, Holmes, stop footling*,' I begged under my breath. '*Tell them.*'

'As a result of our investigations we have discovered something of vital importance about Einstein. It is imperative you should know about it before you offer him employment at your famous University.'

'Which is?' Professor Sobel and the Rector demanded in unison.

'That there is absolutely nothing to report about him. My good friend and I found nothing amiss. Nothing. I think you may fairly go ahead and offer him employment. We trust Albert Einstein will have a long and successful career in science.'

My comrade and I rose as one, stretching out our hands.

Holmes asked, 'If there is no other point to which you would wish to draw our attention...?'

I observed the most profound expression of relief on Professor Sobel's face as he shook his head. In a babble of thanks and chortles and goodbyes we were shown from the office.

**

We were once more on the streets of Berne. A short distance from the university I grasped my comrade's arm, unable to restrain myself any longer.

'Holmes,' I demanded, 'you know perfectly well you did not tell the truth back there. Whatever the mitigating circumstances, however palsied the infant, you yourself concluded that this contemptible scoundrel Einstein was deeply involved in the dispatch – murder – of his daughter.'

Angrily I continued, 'He may not be Lucifer himself, but he is at least the equal of any of the Four Horsemen! Regardless of whatever astounding scientific theory he has just propounded, one word from you to the Rector at this or any other university, and his career in physics would be at an end. For reasons far beyond my comprehension, you failed to report the truth!'

'My dear friend,' came the reply, 'whoever sent those notes had sufficient knowledge to ruin Einstein's career without our investigation. Why then were we needed? When the Professor handed us the first scrap of paper I concluded – wrongly – that someone was intent on preventing Einstein's career from taking off. Perhaps a wronged woman, a jilted lover.'

He frowned. 'Now I realise Zorka's objective lies elsewhere, but where and how we are to proceed? That is the question. And as yet – '

His voice trailed away. The tangle of small streets brought us unexpectedly to the square containing the Café Bollwerk. The tables were refilling with the gaggles of students we had unconsciously been following.

'Then what do we do?' I asked.

'We wait, Watson. We wait.'

We seated ourselves at a table. 'Holmes,' I accosted crossly, 'what have we accomplished? Nothing!'

I repeated, 'We have accomplished nothing. We criss-cross the Danube. We face a host of diseases, any of which would have been fatal to men of our middling age. We rattle around on the worst of cart-tracks, stay in hostelries more run down than any in England since Chaucer's time, and brave a haunted house. Despite all this, the Rector and Professor Sobel know nothing about Lieserl, under what circumstances and to whom she was born, let alone her desperate fate.'

'Patience, my dear Watson,' came Holmes's laconic words. 'We must – ' He broke off, glancing sharply over my shoulder.

'I see we are about to have an interesting encounter with an old friend.'

The now-familiar figure of Professor Sobel was approaching the café at a brisk pace. On catching sight of us he came to an abrupt stop, then waved energetically and hurried towards our table.

'Mr. Holmes, I must thank you from the depths of my heart. Discovering nothing was the finest outcome we could have wished. Dr. Watson, I was on my way to your hotel to deliver this.'

He withdrew an envelope from a pocket. 'I believe this should cover your expenses.'

I reached out a hand to receive the envelope.

As I did so I heard Holmes say, 'You knew the truth all along, didn't you, Professor Sobel?'

Holmes's eyes were fixed on Professor Sobel's as though reading his very soul. Both the Professor and I froze.

'What do you mean, Mr. Holmes?' he asked, a hint of anxiety in his tone.

'Our hotel lies in a quite different direction – you were not on your way there,' came the reply. 'You had no idea Watson and I would be here, at the Café Bollwerk. You expected instead to meet your future *Assistent*, to tell him the good news, that we had discovered nothing. I am certain young Albert is hot-footing it here even as we speak. We told the Rector that there were no skeletons in Einstein's cupboard, but you and I know that was not true.'

'What did you find out?' the Professor asked.

'It will only confirm what I believe you yourself already know,' Holmes replied.

'Namely?'

'That the Lieserl referred to in the first note was Einstein's illegitimate daughter,' Holmes continued. 'That she died a violent death in Serbia aged around twenty-one months.'

The Professor stayed silent for a moment. Finally he asked, 'Why did you choose not to disclose this to the Rector?'

Holmes seemed to reflect for a moment.

Finally he answered, 'On balance, I felt Mileva's well-being and her love for Einstein and their son Hans Albert obliged us to let sleeping dogs lie.'

The Professor broke into a relieved laugh. 'I admit I did know more than I revealed,' he exclaimed. 'Even the Holy Patriarch when hungry will steal a piece of bread. When that first note arrived I confronted Einstein just as I described to you. I said the note had raised serious concern in the Rector's mind and I insisted on knowing who Lieserl might be. I told Albert his entire career was teetering on the edge of the precipice and that my concern had not been quelled by his vehement response to the simple query, *Do you know anyone called Lieserl?* A mild "no", with a polite "I'm afraid not" would have sufficed.'

'Then the second note came,' Holmes prompted.

'Yes. I brought it with me to the Bollwerk and told Einstein of its content.'

'How did he respond?' I enquired.

'The word "Titel" jolted him badly. He promised to take me into his confidence on the condition I would do everything to keep the matter from the Rector's ears.'

'I presume you agreed?' I said.

'I gave him my word.'

'Continue please, Professor,' Holmes ordered.

'Einstein pleaded his case. He told me how hard he had fought to leave home and get into the Zurich *Polytechnikum*, about his struggle with the mathematics. How he wandered into a seminar and saw Mileva, the dark-haired Slav, sitting there, the only female student in the class. How she offered to help him. How they spent more and more time together until he forgot she had a limp and wore an orthopaedic shoe. And how they went secretly to Como in the spring of 1899 and there on the banks of the lake they made love.'

He went on, 'When she realised she was pregnant Mileva begged Albert to let her stay with him here in Berne. He refused. Against her will he sent her back to Novi-Sad to have the child. He said he never saw it before it died.'

'Did he say how the child died?' Holmes asked.

'He swore it was from Scarlet Fever.'

I intervened. 'And you believed him?'

Professor Sobel shrugged and stayed silent.

'Professor,' I asked, my gorge rising, 'if you knew all this, why – ?'

Holmes interrupted: 'You mean, why did our friend send us galloping off to Serbia?'

'That's precisely what I mean.'

Holmes glanced at Professor Sobel.

'Our Professor knows the world of Academe only too well. Accusations of special pleading. The smears, the jostling, the smouldering ambitions, the perpetual hatreds and jealousies. Desperately – more than anything in the world – he wanted Einstein in his Department. He already knew the lad was an analytical genius in the making, even an Isaac Newton, a Kepler. Professor, am I correct in believing Mileva gave you prior knowledge of the equivalence theory Einstein was about to launch on an astounded world?'

The Professor nodded. Holmes looked back to me.

'Professor Sobel also knew from the minute the Rector sanctioned young Einstein's employment in the Physics Department, jealousies would erupt. Rumour-mongering would become rampant. A shadow of distrust would endanger Einstein's position at the University. It could even wreck his career. The Department's reputation would be sullied, the Rector humiliated. Pressed almost beyond endurance, the Professor cast around for a solution. And it was you, Watson, who gave him an opportunity he seized upon with alacrity.'

Before I could make an indignant protest, Holmes continued. 'Professor, Watson's ruse commending me for an *Honoris causa* landed on your desk. Astutely, you realised all rumours about Einstein could be scotched before they arose if the great Sherlock Holmes investigated and found nothing. You were certain the Balkans would defeat us. Einstein's reputation – and your Department's – would be safe for ever.'

Holmes gave a grim smile. 'It was a grave risk you took. It very nearly succeeded. I have said that if I had not become a Consulting Detective, I would have become a scientist. May I say that had you not become a scientist you would have made an excellent Sherlock Holmes.'

'Or a second Moriarty!' I exclaimed, seething with indignation.

'Or a second Moriarty!' Holmes agreed.

Both he and Professor Sobel burst into a roar of laughter at my hot displeasure.

Chapter XIII

Zorka Provides A Weapon Of Exemplary Power

Holmes and I sat together on the balcony of his room at the Hotel Sternen Muri. He was on his third (or was it fourth?) cigar of the morning, blowing little wavering rings of smoke up to the sky. I was ready for our return to England. My luggage contained a Brienz chalet cuckoo-clock with animated woodcutter figurines for Mrs. Hudson's hallway. It would go well with the barometer. Holmes had his Honorary Doctorate certificate. I could see no point in remaining in Switzerland a minute longer.

Finally I burst out, 'Holmes, three days! You have kept us here, waiting, for three whole days! And for what?'

'Patience, my dear Watson,' came the exasperating reply. 'We needed time to let her think it over – '

From the room behind us we heard the sound of approaching footsteps.

'But I believe the wait is over.'

I stood up. An envelope slithered under the door. It contained two letters. Holmes studied the first and moved on to the second. He read it through twice before returning to the first.

'As your German is shaky, Watson, I'll translate. Both these letters were posted from Mileva in Novi-Sad to Albert nearly two years ago. In this one she calls Albert "Johnnie" and signs herself Dollie. She indicates she is *enceinte* – with her son Hans

Albert as it turned out. Not feeling well 'just like the first time' confirms she had been so before.

Friday 19 June 1903
My Dearest Little Johnnie,

Your poor Dollie misses you terribly. It's going quickly, but badly. I'm not feeling well at all, just like the first time. It's so hot even the quail are hiding in the tall grass. Here I am, stuck in stinky Novi-Sad, dreaming I am walking in the cool Bernese Alps in the arms of my beloved sweetheart, amid the Asters and Rock Jasmine. It's getting very humid. My mother has just evicted our cat. To avoid bad luck, a black cat must be ejected from the house whenever there's thunder in the air.

So many superstitions rule our lives in Serbia. Whether the cocks crow in unison, the dogs bark much (or not at all), the frogs croak. Sorceries are practiced when a woman has no children. People with blue eyes are more likely to have the Evil Eye. The American painter Holman Hunt had difficulty in getting Serbs to sit for him, despite the offer of a most handsome fee. On Judgement Day they feared their portrait might arrive at the Gates of Heaven before them. When the Holy Archangel arrived with the sitter's soul, Saint Peter would wave the soul away as an imposter. I really do laugh internally, but I don't want to offend my dear family by giggling out loud at their backward beliefs. As to burial customs among our mountain brethren – my supply of writing-paper is running too low to go into those.

There is a superstition I hold to because it is beautiful. Each person is assigned a star which appears in the sky at the exact moment of his birth and will snuff out for ever when he dies. On our birth certificates even to-day we put the hour as well as the day. My sweet little treasure, when I am back in Switzerland we must buy a good telescope and take it up the Gurten and search out your star. I know you were born on the 14th of March 1879. Can you discover from your mother the exact hour, even the minute?

I am doing as you ordered, fattening up so that I will rest against you once more, plump as a dumpling and healthy and cheerful. My 'peasant' diet consists largely of wheat bread and *pasulj*, a thick gruel made of beans boiled in water until pulpy, and potato and pepper stews. Sometimes we have *gibanica* which one day I shall bake for you.

How my heart will pound when I next see your open arms! I'll be so proud and happy when we are together again and can bring our work on relative motion to a successful conclusion.

We have a saying, "Life gives to every slave an empty glass to fill either with tears or with hope". Mine is a quarter full (of tears).

My mother is calling to me. Please write very soon.

Think a bit about your little one, and be hugged and kissed by your Dollie.'

'What a truly affectionate letter, Holmes,' I cried.

'As you say, Watson, a truly affectionate letter, but it gives us no clue as to what Zorka requires of us. However, I believe we shall find our answer in this second letter.'

He added, 'This time Mileva signs herself Doxerl.' He unfolded the single page.

'Friday 26th June 1903 Novi-Sad
My dearest little sweetheart,

Your letters from Schaffhausen told me you doubted the correctness of our ideas about relative motion. Your reservations are due to a simple mistake in the numerical calculation. The value for the mass of the sun is off by a factor of 10.

You told me of your struggles with the mass-energy equivalence problem. I locked myself up and I believe I have found the answer. I've come to the conclusion that mass is a direct measure for the energy contained in bodies, so light transfers mass. If a body releases the rest mass energy L in the form of radiation, its mass is diminished by L/V^2, thereby we come to the formula $L=mV^2$.

I hope you have had time to do more work on frames of reference in uniform relative motion with respect to each other. Shall we call it Special Theory? I am certain it will make you world famous. How all the universities will clamour to employ you, even stuffy Berne.

When you are famous, I shall look forward to lying in your arms once more on a little holiday. I have often heard the adage "I was so happy I wish I'd died". Those were my feelings when we were on our first holiday together in

Como and made love on the banks. Do you remember when we boarded that bright white steamer and heard the sound of church bells across the water? The Italians told us the peals were for the fishermen pulling black eels and grey herrings from the lake, but I know they were not. The bells were for us.

A *Fijaker* is stationed outside our front door all day, ready for a quick departure. My father is thinking to remove the family to the mountains to escape the scarlet fever. Now that he understands how much I love you, I am sure he has forgiven you for being a Swab. A Jew is fine with him. Our family Saint, Stefan the Martyr, was born a Jew. We are in it together. Everyone looks down on Jews and everyone looks down on us Serbs too.

A thousand kisses from your poor lonely Doxerl.

Ps. Next we must formulate equations of the gravitational field.'

'Holmes,' I exclaimed, 'I fail to see how these letters add to our knowledge. The one is a letter from a woman deeply in love with a husband many hundreds of miles away. The second talks about a scientific theory they've clearly been discussing for quite some time. And now Einstein has published that formula in the *Annalen der Physik.*'

Holmes threw the letters towards me with a triumphant gesture. 'The first letter confirms how deeply Mileva loves Einstein. At the very least Zorka is warning us not to do anything to destroy the lad's career or shatter the marriage. That was never her intent. But this second letter – why do you suppose Zorka has sent it to us?'

'As I say, I presume she ... '

'Presume nothing, Watson – *think*! We come back to the question I asked myself time and again, what is it Zorka really wants? What was her reason for leading us to the grave-pit?'

I shook my head. 'I am quite out of my depth, Holmes.'

'I believe I have the answer, Watson. It was you who gave me the clue. Do you recall making use of your compass at the burial site? What was it you discovered?'

'That the skeleton lay roughly on a north-east axis?'

'And therefore?'

'It was not a Christian burial.'

'So let me recapitulate. By leading us to the grave, Zorka believed she was handing us a sword of Damocles, though for what purpose we had no idea. The moment we entered Professor Sobel's office on our return from Titel I realised – just in time - there was an insuperable flaw. Revealing the circumstances of Lieserl's life and especially her death would lead where? Einstein would hotly refute any knowledge whatsoever of the matter. Who would contradict him? Miloš Marić? He lifted himself up from the peasantry to a position in society which he would not willingly throw away. He could be found guilty of murder and shot in open ground. He will say nothing. Zorka? That *mirna ludakinja*? Mileva? It could wreck her husband's career and Steinli's future. Professor Sobel and the Rector? Absolutely not – they are beside themselves with glee at the prospect of clasping this genius to their bosom.'

Holmes tapped the second letter.

'Whatever her plan, if we were to carry it out, Zorka had to provide us with a weapon of exemplary power – and she has. This letter proves that two years ago Mileva – not Albert –

arrived at the mass-energy relation. We only have to release the letter to the *Annalen der Physik* and the world will rank Mileva alongside Newton in the pantheon of science, far above Einstein. Do you think for one instant the young man's monumental ego will permit this?'

'Holmes,' I replied, 'not for the first time in our adventures together I struggle in your wake. Zorka may have handed us a weapon of great power but if it isn't to expose Einstein for the rogue he patently is, why did she make us ride the whirlwind?'

'I shall now reveal all in a letter of our own, Watson. Take down the following.'

'Herrn Albert Einstein, 3rd Floor Swiss Patents Office, corner of Speichergasse and Genfergasse, Berne. Personal. Dear Sir, the mass-energy equivalence formulation $L=mV^2$ merits the applause of the scientific world. The clockwork tapestry put together by the physicists of the enlightenment will unravel at the claim that Gravity and acceleration are essentially one, that a time-piece located at the Equator must run slower than one at the poles. The creator of such a far-reaching formulation truly deserves a place in the pantheon of science. History will credit your name unless evidence comes to light to challenge your possession of that accolade.'

Holmes waited while I caught up. 'You ask after Zorka's goal, Watson – I shall now tell you. Please continue with our letter:

'You will have heard that Dr. Watson and I recently visited Titel. We return with a request from Lieserl. So she may face eternity with equanimity, the infant wishes to be taken from the pit she's in and laid to rest in holy ground … '

My comrade broke off.

'Where would you suggest, Watson? Under the care of the Archimandrite?'

'Or Father Florus?' I suggested, adding mischievously, 'it's a trek longer and twice as arduous as the climb to the Reichenbach Falls.'

'Our Lady Among the Rocks – where else!' Holmes exclaimed.

Had he discovered a gold mine, greater delight could not have shone upon my companion's features.

'Good! Excellent, Watson! Continue:

'at the Church of Our Lady Among the Rocks'.

'Put a map-reference there.'

Holmes stopped to give me an enquiring look. 'Which flowers shall we command this Einstein to place on his daughter's grave?'

'In our long years together, Holmes, you mentioned only one flower, the moss-rose,' I replied.

'The moss-rose it is! Write as follows:

'We are quite certain you will be able to arrange this simple matter. Please ensure personally that the grave-site is strewn annually with the moss-rose. It blooms all summer.

May I congratulate you on the prospective offer of a position in Professor Sobel's Department.'

And, with its hint of menace, Watson, end the letter with:

'We shall monitor your career with very great interest.
I am,
Very sincerely etc.
S. Holmes.'

At this my companion leapt to his feet.

'Hats, Baedeker and your Gladstone, Watson! Leave the letter at the hotel desk for posting. That should do it. The chase is at an end. Einstein will know at once the threat which confronts him. He knows we shall stay silent only if he carries out his side of the bargain. Otherwise, the world of science will have a scandal on its hands beyond the Rector's wildest fears.'

162

Chapter XIV

The Matter Settled, We Return to Baker Street

We were on our way home. Holmes and I sat across from each other in a swiftly-moving railway carriage, he in his long grey travelling-coat and deerstalker cap, Bradshaw's *Railway Guide* at his side, Gladstone bag at mine. Paris had come and gone. Ahead lay Calais. Our concern that agents from Moran's criminal gang would lie in wait for us at Calais or the white cliffs of Dover had dissipated with the weeks spent in Serbia. Soon we would be greeted by our loyal Mrs. Hudson on that fine street laid out by master builder William Baker, nestled in the splendour and squalor of England's Capital city, over it all the comforting sound of a bell striking from a distant tower.

My comrade filled a pipe and applied a flame. He looked across at me through the fumes.

'The fair sex is your department, Watson,' he said reflectively, 'but women never cease to amaze me. So profound is Mileva's love for Einstein that, unless her own letter was thrust before her on the witness stand, I am certain she would affirm in a Court of Law, even on the Holy Bible, that it was her husband and he alone who formulated the magical equation on which he may now build a considerable career.'

His voice softened. 'I am satisfied we did what was required of us. If Lieserl is not reburied in hallowed ground, Zorka believes the child will continue to live out her natural term as a *rusalka*. By obliging young Einstein to go, however secretly, to Titel and arrange the reburial of his daughter in holy ground, we may have done him a considerable favour. If the matter had festered in Zorka's mind much longer, the crime she might have committed against his person can only be left to the mists of conjecture. The infant is beyond our powers of reassurance, but it is all men's wish to see justice done, especially to the dead. Lieserl will rest sheltered by Father Florus and the Hand of God. Once done, the *rusalka* will fall silent, the haunted house will become a simple ruin.'

Holmes looked at me reflectively. 'They may call Zorka *mirna ludakinja* as much as they wish, but she has a remarkable mind. Her enterprise was done brilliantly. She led everyone to believe her old home was haunted, while the matter of Lieserl's final resting place awaited settlement. She has ensured the reburial of an infant in a quiet and beautiful spot, in sacred ground. As to Mileva, due fame has been withheld from her, but she knows there are always those who despise and fear profoundly any women with a mind the equal or greater of men. Had we revealed the truth, it might not have benefitted her in her lifetime. The hyenas would slip their leash. Her enemies would call her an adventuress, a liar, a cheat, a *grande horizontale*. At least you and I know the truth.'

He glanced across at me.

'Until you choose to publish this adventure we must console ourselves that the secret history of the world is frequently so much more interesting than the public chronicles.'

I asked, 'How do you suppose Zorka gained possession of those letters?'

'Given Einstein's disinclination to acknowledge anyone but himself in the new theories, I suggest he thought he had long since been rid of them. It's entirely conceivable that Zorka went through his waste-paper basket not long after they were discarded and squirreled them away for a rainy day.'

'And that rainy day came.'

'It did.'

Holmes's eyes twinkled.

'Now we can return to Mrs. Hudson's dinners. As to whether we regale her with fishing tales from the Tisza … '

I nodded, pondering another matter. My own commission had failed. How was I to break the news to Sir George Newnes?

Holmes sensed my abstraction.

'My dear friend, you have not brought up the matter which must surely be very close to your heart and certainly to your pocket.'

'Which is, Holmes?' I enquired as innocently as I could.

'The Christmas cover photograph for the *Strand*.'

'Ah,' I responded. '*That* matter! I had quite forgotten.'

He tapped me on the knee. 'When we get back to London I shall commission John Singer Sargent to paint an Alpine waterfall – one of his six-footers. As soon as you purchase a camera, and if my clothes ever dry, I shall pose for you in front of Mr. Sargent's backcloth of roiling waters, safe in the heart of the Sussex Downs.'

We continued in this happy vein while our train chugged through the long twilight.

Once more in London, an excited Mrs Hudson greeted us. She handed me a telegram. It was from Colonel Moran. We read it silently.

'To Messrs. Holmes and Watson. 31st May 05. Trent Bridge. Englands cricketers under Stanley Jackson beat

165

Australia by 213 runs. Bosanquet's googlies took 8 Australian wickets for 107 runs second innings.

I am sending you two tickets for Lords August 2nd.

Col Sebastian Moran

'Aha! He's back!' Holmes exclaimed. 'He kept his vile hounds at bay in order to challenge us to a duel. The wheel grinds ever onward.'

As I climbed the steep stairway to our rooms Holmes called back, 'What takes place at Lord's Cricket Ground on August 2nd, Watson?'

'The centenary Eton versus Harrow match,' I replied.

'We have something to look forward to. Our Colonel will want to redress the humiliation we've just inflicted upon on him, no matter what the cost to his well-being.'

'Or to his life,' I added, reaching the landing. I pointed at Holmes's pocket containing the hip-pocket Webley.

'We shall be ready, Holmes,' I said confidently. 'If he dares to tangle with us at Lord's, even on the Mound, he will quickly find himself on the London Necropolis Line with a one-way ticket to Brookwood Cemetery.'

'Watson,' Holmes said, unable to repress a smile, 'no-one can say you are just a galumphing St. Bernard. There is something of the Kipling in you. May I interest you in a Trichinopoly cheroot?'

'My dear Holmes, I would rather smoke an Old Bailey judge's Full Bottom horsehair wig.'

Postscript

In 1907, two years after the publication of the paper, Einstein changed the first formulation L=mV² to E=MC², the most famous equation in physics. Over the following decades the esteem, even reverence, accorded this remarkable scientist, stemming from the *Annus Mirabilis* of 1905, became unstoppable. Had Holmes revealed his deduction to the world at that time, that this Newton incarnate had fathered an illegitimate child who was then subjected to a mercy-killing, it is no exaggeration to say that, rather than ending Einstein's career before it had begun, Holmes and Watson might themselves have become objects of derision, even of dangerous hatreds.

Holmes and Watson's experience in Serbia was far from wasted. What they learnt in the search for Lieserl was to be of extraordinary value when, hardly a year later, at the behest of Britain's Foreign Secretary, Sir Edward Grey, Holmes and Watson paid a second visit to Constantinople on a most secret and sensitive mission concerning the Sword of Osman. The great Islamic Empire, which the Romanovs memorably dubbed the 'Sick Man of Europe' was collapsing. Was an uprising against the Caliph in the offing? And with what consequence for Britain's interests in the Middle East and India? More to the point, what devious part was Mycroft about to play in the proceedings?

Endnotes

The Cullinan Diamond was named after Sir Thomas Cullinan, the mine-owner. At 3,106-carats, contemporary estimates of its value, if cut into a dozen marketable stones, were around GB£150,000, the equivalent in to-day's money of GB£45 million. The stone was bought by the Transvaal government and presented to King Edward VII on his birthday. The task of transporting the stone to London involved a diversionary tactic worthy of Holmes. The rumour was deliberately spread that the diamond was being transported to England on a steamboat, with detectives crammed aboard. The stone on board was a glass replica. The real diamond was sent to England in a plain box via parcel post (albeit registered).

James McParland. The Pinkerton agent in Conan Doyle's *The Valley of Fear*, the fourth and final Sherlock Holmes novel, was supposedly based on the real-life exploits of Pinkerton agent James McParland and the Molly Maguires.

Watson's Army career in India and Afghanistan commenced with a medical degree from the University of London. The college validated credentials earned through hospital study, rather than offering medical instruction of its own.

Strand Magazine. Except for the first two Sherlock Holmes novels, all the detective stories had their first UK publication in the *Strand*, a monthly magazine founded at the beginning of 1891 by Sir George Newnes, the creator (in 1881) of *Tit-Bits*, the weekly paper of miscellaneous information and entertainment. The *Strand* was introduced as a more respectable product, with the title taken from the fashionable West End thoroughfare. Issues often contained short stories translated from the French or Russian, and it was – for Conan Doyle – a mark of success that his stories were included in this prestigious publication.

The Ghost of Grosvenor Square. By failing to explain this interesting case, Watson does himself a disservice. After being shown around the site of a crime, a Mayfair mansion, he deduced the intruder was garrotted by a sightless man who knew the house well. Scotland Yard put out an international arrest order for the mansion's owner, an American, who had fled the country and was indeed blind.

The Criterion, a famous restaurant located near Piccadilly Circus. Arthur Conan Doyle set a very early meeting (late 1880 or early 1881) between Holmes and Watson in the Criterion Long Bar, later a convenient meeting spot for the Suffragettes.

'Napoleon Crossing the St. Bernard'. A propaganda painting by Jacque-Louis David, depicting Napoleon in his famous crossing of the Alps. In reality, Napoleon crossed the Alps on a mule, not a magnificent horse. Mules have better balance and traction, are lower to the ground, and do better in cold weather.

The Prince Regnant of Bulgaria. A central character in *Sherlock Holmes and The Case of The Bulgarian Codex,* where Holmes was commissioned to find a stolen ancient manuscript of very considerable ceremonial and political importance.

Hegira. Migration of the Islamic prophet Muhammad and his followers from Mecca to Medina, here used as 'journey'.

Rara avis. A rare or unique person or thing.

Redresseur de destins. A rectifier of destinies.

Junior United Service Club. A gentleman's club in London founded in 1827 and based at 11 Charles Street. Membership was restricted to former or serving officers in the Navy or Army with at least five years active service. Unlike its senior, the United Services Club in Pall Mall, its fees were moderate, which was why it was attractive to Dr Watson.

Doctor Honoris Causa. Honorary Doctorate. These started to be granted by universities across Europe (including Oxford and Cambridge) in the fifteenth century. The ceremony usually includes a eulogistic statement in Latin and/or Greek by the University Orator, justifying the grant, opening with the word 'Whereas' and the concluding statement with 'Therefore'. Those granted doctorates '*honoris causa*' do not usually thereafter term themselves Doctor unless they have a separate academic doctorate. In November 1919, on the celebration of the 500th anniversary of the University of Rostock, Albert Einstein and Max Planck (German physicist and Nobel laureate, 1858-1947) were awarded honorary doctorates, Einstein for Medicine 'in recognition of the enormous work of his mind', the only honorary doctorate Einstein was given in Germany. He was granted a doctorate '*honoris causa*' by Princeton University in 1921 and by Oxford in 1931.

'Drumming a tattoo on his knee with his fingers'. This tell-tale habit has been used by several authors to give the villain away. For instance, Sir Edmund Appleton in Scottish author John Buchan's *The Thirty-Nine Steps*, the first of five novels featuring Richard Hannay. Hannay was an all-action hero with a stiff upper lip and a miraculous knack for getting himself out of sticky situations.

Penang Lawyer. A walking stick made of the stem of an East Asiatic palm (*Licuala acutifida*). Its bulbous head was hollowed out and filled with lead, making it a formidable weapon.

2/8d and 3/6d. Two shillings and eight pence, i.e. two pennies over a half-crown. Some calculations estimate the purchasing power of 2/8d in 1905 as approximately GB£41.74 or US$67.64 in 2014. Three shillings and sixpence – calculations based on the purchasing power of 3/6d suggest its purchasing power would be GB£54.78 or US$88.77.

The double rifle. This Victorian development excels over other repeating firearms by allowing a split-second, secondary shot without having to work the firearm's action. As I myself discovered when farming in East Africa, this can be a matter of life or death for the shooter when a large, dangerous animal chooses to charge, especially in close quarters or in thick cover. The double rifle rapidly became the weapon-of-choice of many professional White Hunters in India and especially in Africa, and still is.

Tractarian. Members of the Anglican High Church movement were also sometimes known as Tractarians. This High Church link in Watson's background is not widely known. Here, in prompting a Nonconformist clergyman (let alone Sherlock Holmes) to display Biblical knowledge based on the Old Testament, he was being mischievous. Many Nonconformist ministers had never been to Oxford or Cambridge and were not likely therefore to have the detailed knowledge of the Scriptures in their original formats. Holmes had to choose a *Nonconformist* clergyman or a Catholic priest - at that time, to impersonate a minister of the Church of England was a criminal offence under the English Law, while to impersonate any other clergyman - i.e., any minister of a cult different from the official religion of the State - was not.

Churchwarden clay pipes. These are characterised by an extremely long stem, up to 20 inches in length.

The Colonial and Continental Church Society. A Protestant missionary society, created by the amalgamation of two early nineteenth century societies in 1851. It specialised in sending out clerically-qualified schoolmasters and catechists to areas such as Catholic Europe and Russia as well as North America, unlike the better-known societies such as the Church Missionary Society which specialised in locations outside Europe.

Norfolk Suit. During the Edwardian period, the Norfolk jacket remained fashionable for shooting and rugged outdoor pursuits. Made of sturdy tweed or similar fabric, it featured paired box pleats over the chest and back, with a fabric belt. When worn with matching breeches (U.S. knickerbockers), it became the Norfolk suit, with knee-length stockings and shoes suitable for bicycling or golf, or for hunting with sturdy boots or shoes with leather gaiters.

The pictorial postcard. This was introduced into Britain in 1894 and became particularly popular with Edwardians throughout the Empire, including India. In Britain, most were sold for a half-penny. With up to ten deliveries a day in urban areas, it was nearly as synchronous as the Twitter and Twitpic of to-day and often as relaxed and conversational in tone. As late as 1908 a priggish character in a story remarked: 'I have always been brought up to think it rather rude to send postcards, unless they are picture ones for people to put in their albums'.

Frederick Scholte. Tailoring was softened in the early twentieth century by Savile Row's Frederick Scholte, especially when he developed the English drape. Scholte became the Duke of Windsor's (King Edward VIII's) tailor. The Duke commented 'Scholte had rigid standards concerning the perfect balance of proportions between shoulders and waist in the cut of a coat to clothe the masculine torso . . . . These peculiar proportions were Scholte's secret formula.'

'Omnis intellectualis scientia' etc. Aristotle. *Metaphysics*, v. 1. Translates roughly as 'All intellectual knowledge, whether or not generated by him, is concerned with its causes and the principles behind its rules.'

Olympia Academy. Einstein met regularly to read and discuss books on science and philosophy with other friends in Bern, all yet unknown to the academic world. They called themselves the Olympia Academy, mocking the official bodies that dominated science.

Blackstone's Commentaries on the Law of England. Holmes would have known that this famous law book was utilised by the American 'traitor' General Benedict Arnold during the War of Independence, to communicate messages intended for British eyes.

Michele Besso. Until only a few years before his death, Einstein was – to put it mildly – frugal in acknowledging the work of others in the field, including contemporaries such as Jules Henri Poincaré. The one exception was life-long friend, engineer Michele Besso, valuable to Einstein as a sounding board. This earned Besso the famous acknowledgment in the special relativity paper of 1905. Nevertheless, Besso's help in a technical problem concerning Einstein's paper on the perihelion problem was never publicly acknowledged. Einstein did not know at that point that his friend and admirer Besso would preserve these earlier calculations for posterity.

Gemütlich. The term is often argued to be difficult to translate, but the broad sense is that it represents something or someone comfortable, cosy or easy, with whom one could be informal.

Displaced hip. As Michele Zackheim points out in *Einstein's Daughter: The Search for Lieserl*, Mileva Marić's displaced hip was a congenital condition widespread in the Balkans, occurring in more than a fifth of the population, mostly female and mostly the left hip.

The ambitious Einstein. Einstein was notably ambitious from extreme youth. Describing the Einstein about to take up the post at the Swiss Patents Office, Biographer Albrecht Fölsing wrote, 'There probably never was a young man about to enter a modest post with, at the same time, such high-flying plans as Albert Einstein, when he arrived in Bern in February 1902.' Fölsing added, 'And the most astonishing thing is that his hopes came true.'

Anti-Semitism. In my novels set in the Edwardian period such as *the Mystery of Einstein's Daughter* I have portrayed Holmes' and Dr. Watson's attitudes towards the Jews as standard for their period. There is little material in Conan Doyle's works indicating the pair was closely acquainted with anyone of Jewish descent. In *The Adventure of Shoscombe Old Place* the word Jew is synonymous with moneylender, a usage dating from the Middle Ages when only Jews were allowed to be bankers in the Christian world. Holmes is said to have bought his Stradivarius violin from a 'Jew broker' in the Tottenham Court Road.

-ić. Most Serbian surnames (like Bosnian, Croatian and Montenegrin) have the surname suffix -ić This is often transliterated as -ic or -ici. In history, Serbian names have often been transcribed with a phonetic ending, -ich or -itch. This form is often associated with Serbs from before the early 20th century. Hence a name like Milanković would usually be referred to, for historical reasons, as Milankovitch.

Scarlet Fever. This was the most dreaded form of streptococcal infection. Simply hearing the name and knowing it was present in the community was enough to strike fear. Even when not fatal, the disease caused large amounts of suffering to those infected. In the worst cases, all of a family's children could die over the course of a week or two. Dr. Charles Tait, later Archbishop of Canterbury, lost five of his six children within a month in 1856.

Marionette Shows/Puppetry. As yet undetermined, puppetry may have originated in India about 4,000 years ago. In Sanskrit plays, the narrator is called *'Sutradhar'* or 'holder of strings,' which is similar to a puppeteer. Early Indian puppet shows dealt with religious themes and political satires. By 1730, Japanese puppetry had become so complex that each puppet had to be operated by three puppeteers. Puppets made their first emergence in Europe through Greece. Puppet plays were shown at the Theatre of Dionysus at Acropolis. This gave rise to the *Commedia dell'arte* tradition. Italian marionette shows produced tragedies like 'Dr. Faust'. For centuries, puppetry catered for adults rather than children. In Victorian Britain adult works were overshadowed by the violent Punch and Judy shows for children's entertainment. Nowadays puppetry very much includes works for adults, for example the National Bunraku Puppet Theatre in Osaka, which has developed the art of *ningyo joruri Bunraku*, specifically adult drama. See www.osaka-info.jp/en/search/detail/sightseeing_1953.html.

Marionette. A puppet controlled from above using wires or strings. The term is used to distinguish theatre of this nature from other forms such as finger, glove, and shadow puppetry and is derived from 'little Mary' – one of the first figures to be made into a marionette was the Virgin Mary. A marionette's puppeteer is called a manipulator. Puppets performances, although already popular in the early 1600s, became the primary theatrical medium in England in 1642. When Cromwell and the Puritans governed the Commonwealth, theatre doors were locked tight. The marionettes kept playing because they did not seem important enough to ban. From 1642 until a couple of years after Cromwell's death in 1658, puppet theatre was the only public entertainment on offer. See www.currentmiddleages.org/artsci/docs/Champ_Bane_Marionette.pdf.

Tarantass. A low-slung, four-wheeled carriage, common in Russia and also found in other parts of eastern Europe.

Rusalka. This translates as a female ghost, associated with the unquiet dead who died violently

Oracle at Delphi. From wikispaces: 'Oracles were believed to have unique access to the gods of a particular religion and through this access were often able to see into the future. The most revered oracle in ancient Greece was located at the town of Delphi in the temple of Apollo, the god of prophecy. The prestige of this oracle made Delphi the most important, influential, and wealthy sacred place in the entire Greek world.

'For at least a thousand years, the pronouncements of the Delphic oracle offered divine guidance on issues ranging from the founding of colonies to declarations of war, as well as advice on personal issues. Rulers of Greece, Persia, and the Roman Empire made the arduous journey to this mountainous site.'

See http://farrington1600.wikispaces.com/file/view/ Delphic Oracle.pdf

Edith Durham. In *the Mystery of Einstein's Daughter,* Miss Durham is found happily painting in Serbia. In real life, she was considered the century's prime interpreter of Albania. According to Charles King (*Times Literary Supplement*, 4 August 2000, pp. 13-14) she was 'the most important writer on that culture since J. C. Hobhouse journeyed through the Albanian lands with Byron.' She was adored among the Albanians themselves, who knew her as *Kralica e Malësorevet* – the Queen of the Highlanders.

Jacob and Wilhelm Grimm. The Brothers Grimm were nineteenth century German nationalists, who used their academic and linguistic skills to travel through 'Germany' (then more a geographical than a political state term), collecting folk tales to show the cultural unity of Germany. From their tales, we have such stories as Hansel and Gretel, Rumpelstiltskin and Snow White.

The Pig War. Also known as the Customs War, this was an economic conflict which really did take place between the Habsburg Empire and the Kingdom of Serbia in 1906-1909, in which the Habsburgs imposed a customs blockade on Serbian pork. The conflict was crucial in escalating tensions between the two sides in the early twentieth century, running up to the decision of the Habsburg Empire on a final (and ultimately unsuccessful) military strike at Serbia in 1914, leading to the assassination at Sarajevo of Archduke Franz Ferdinand, the overt cause of World War I.

The Edalji case. George Edalji was a half-British, half-Indian lawyer solicitor from the West Midlands who became world-famous in 1907 when Sir Arthur Conan Doyle campaigned to have him declared innocent of maliciously mutilating a pony. Edalji was of Parsee heritage on his father's side. It was partially as a result of this case that the Court of Criminal Appeal was established in 1907, so Conan Doyle not only proved Edalji innocent, his work helped establish a way to correct other miscarriages of justice. It is discussed in *Crime News in Modern Britain* by Judith Rowbotham, Kim Stevenson and Samantha Pegg (Palgrave Macmillan, 2013).

Paul Verlaine. Verlaine was a French poet, writing at the end of the nineteenth century (he died in 1896). He is most strongly associated with the Symbolist movement. His poetry (as well as his lifestyle) was considered 'decadent'. Towards the end of his life he converted to Roman Catholicism. By the 1890s he was considered the 'Prince of Poets' by his French peers.

In bocca un lupo!. Italian expression, 'In the mouth of a wolf,' meaning good luck. Clearly Edith Durham is a polyglot.

'Si non è vero, è ben trovato.' '(Even) if it isn't true, it's well contrived.'

Enceinte. Pregnant. Respectable remnants of Victorian England considered it vulgar to use the word 'pregnant', and *enceinte* was preferred in polite circles.

Three-Body Problem. The challenge in taking a set of data that specifies the positions, masses and velocities of three bodies and determining the motions of those bodies. Historically, the first specific three-body problem to receive extended study involved the Moon, Earth and Sun.

Love Letters between Mileva and Albert Einstein. Though those included in this tale were composed for the purpose, there are surviving letters between the two which enabled the use of this narrative device as a key element in the plot. The surviving letters are now in the Albert Einstein Archives, Edmund J Safra Campus, Hebrew University, Jerusalem.

John Singer Sargent. American artist hugely popular in the Edwardian period. He completed the oil *A Parisian Beggar-Girl* in 1880 in the Realism style. A favourite model of his, Carmela Bertagna, was probably the sitter. In 1910 Sargent did paint a waterfall, probably in the Tyrol.

1905. This was the year which saw Einstein's invention of the mass-energy equation in its original form L=mV² (he rewrote it as E=MC² in a 1907 paper). 1905 was to become known in Physics as Einstein's *Annus Mirabilis*, like Isaac Newton's *Annus Mirabilis* of 1666. Launching Special Relativity on a startled world did not bring the 26-year-old Einstein instant fame, and certainly not wealth, because of lack of proof to satisfy the many Doubting Thomases, including the Nobel Committee. Among scientists, with two or three notable exceptions such as Max Planck and H.A. Lorentz, the remarkable papers Einstein rolled out during the year roused long-lived opposition, even hostility, especially over the two concerning Special Theory. This resentment existed among many of the Elders of the European scientific Establishment, not just among paid-up members of the 'Anti-Relativity Company' such as the German anti-Semites, Philipp Lenard and Johannes Stark, with their Nazi-inspired loathing for 'Jewish Physics'. Einstein's Special Theory, later known as Special Relativity, would not be confirmed until well into the 1930s. Eventually, Relativity became one of the two pillars of modern physics, alongside quantum mechanics. It is still a source of wonderment that the twenty-six year old Albert Einstein produced such astounding theories. Hermann Minkowski was Einstein's maths professor at the Zurich Polytechnic, later a professor at Göttingen. He told professional colleagues, 'I really wouldn't have thought Einstein capable' of such work.

A Century later, as Quantum Mechanics developed from Einstein's ideas, Professor Sobel – rather than using the clock ticking away at the poles as an example of Einstein's theories - might have befuddled poor old Watson with this explanation concerning the Schrödinger Equation: 'To put it simply, Dr. Watson, the wavefunction will suddenly change into one or other of the eigenfunctions making it up. This is known as the collapse of the wavefunction and the probability of the wavefunction collapsing into a particular eigenfunction depends on how much that eigenfunction contributed to the original superposition. More precisely, the probability that a given eigenfunction will be chosen is proportional to the square of the coefficient of that eigenfunction in the superposition, normalised so that the overall probability of collapse is unity (i.e. the sum of the squares of all the coefficients is 1). Is that clear?'

The Tesla Memorial Society of New York has campaigned for many years for recognition of the part Mileva Marić played in Relativity and more widely in Einstein's *Annus Mirabilis* of 1905. See www.teslasociety.com/Mileva.htm.

Albert Einstein married Mileva Marić in a Berne Register office in January 1903 when their daughter, Lieserl, was a year old. Effectively, this legitimised the daughter under Swiss law, but Einstein refused to have her brought to Berne. By 1912 Einstein tired of Mileva, becoming contemptuous and rude towards her. He demanded a divorce and Mileva refused. In 1919, Einstein gained her consent by promising her the money from the Nobel Prize it was widely anticipated he would win. Einstein immediately married his cousin Elsa. The Nobel Prize came in 1921 'for his services to Theoretical Physics, and especially for his discovery of the law of the photoelectric effect'. In return for financial support, Einstein seems to have stipulated that Mileva would never discuss their past scientific work with anyone, otherwise financial support would cease. Mileva spent most of the money she received from Albert in bringing up their two sons, Hans Albert and Eduard, especially after Eduard developed severe schizophrenia as a young adult and needed extensive hospitalisation for the rest of his life. In later years, exchanges between Albert and Mileva grew more cordial. Following a series of debilitating strokes, she died in Zurich in 1948. Her obituary did not mention Albert. Einstein died in New Jersey seven years later. In 2005 Mileva Marić was honoured in Zurich by the ETH (the former Zurich Polytechnikum).

Rózsika (Zorka) Marić in real life began increasingly to live up to the description 'loony'. Her father stored a large amount of money out of sight in an abandoned wood stove in the back garden. One day, when no-one was around, Zorka started a fire in the stove and the money was lost in its entirety. Some years later, Mileva went to a court to have her sister certified as an incompetent. Zorka died on a pile of straw at her home. She had left mounds of food and buckets of water for her forty-three cats.

Dr. Johann Büttikofer did exist and he did get an Honorary degree from Berne for trekking into the Liberian interior and discovering the first complete pygmy hippopotamus specimens known to science. He donated them to the Natural History Museum of Leiden.

Lieserl's grave-site has never been found. The author believes she was buried secretly under the porch of one of the former Marić family homes as portrayed in this novel. Perhaps one day a team of forensic scientists will search the gardens of the three houses owned at the time by the Marić family.

Arthur Conan Doyle Stories Mentioned in
Einstein's Daughter

'The Adventure of the Naval Treaty', *Memoirs of Sherlock Holmes* (George Newnes, 1894). Episode XXIII in the *Strand Magazine*, 'Adventures of Sherlock Holmes', the case took place in 1893. Dr. Watson refers a letter to Holmes from an old schoolmate, now a Foreign Office employee from Woking, who has had an important naval treaty stolen from his office.

'The Five Orange Pips', *The Adventures of Sherlock Holmes* (George Newnes, 1892). Episode V in the *Strand Magazine* 'Adventures of Sherlock Holmes', it appeared in November 1891. Conan Doyle later ranked the story seventh in a list of his twelve favourite Sherlock Holmes stories. A young Sussex gentleman named John Openshaw has a strange story: in 1869 his uncle Elias Openshaw had abruptly returned to England to settle on an estate in Sussex after living for many years as a planter in Florida and serving as a Colonel in the Confederate Army. It commences in truly classic Watson fashion: 'When I glance over my notes and records of the Sherlock Holmes cases between the years '82 and '90, I am faced by so many which present strange and interesting features that it is no easy matter to know which to choose and which to leave.'

'The Adventure of the Dying Detective', *His Last Bow. Some Later Reminiscences of Sherlock Holmes* (John Murray, 1917), appearing in the *Strand Magazine* in December 1913. Now back in medical practice, Watson is called to 221B Baker Street to tend Holmes, who is apparently dying of a rare Asian disease contracted while he was on a case at Rotherhithe. Mrs. Hudson says that he has had nothing to eat or drink in three days. Watson is shocked, having heard nothing about his friend's illness. Although widely considered among the lesser of Doyle's 56 Sherlock Holmes short stories, as always it contains nuggets such as the opening lines: 'Mrs. Hudson, the landlady of Sherlock Holmes, was a long-suffering woman. Not only was her first-floor flat invaded at all hours by throngs of singular and often undesirable characters but her remarkable lodger showed an eccentricity and irregularity in his life which must have sorely tried her patience'.

'The Adventure of the Illustrious Client', *The Casebook of Sherlock Holmes* (John Murray, 1927), appearing in the *Strand Magazine* in two parts in February and March 1925. Sir James Damery, presumably of legal fame, comes to see Holmes and Watson about an illustrious client's problem (the client's identity is never revealed, although Watson finds out at the end of the story). Old General de Merville's daughter, Violet, has fallen madly in love with Austrian Baron Adelbert Gruner. Both Sir James and Holmes are convinced that the Baron is a murderer, the victim being his last wife, who met her end in the Splügen Pass. He was acquitted of her murder because of a legal technicality and a witness's untimely death. Wonderful lines from it include 'Both Holmes and I had a weakness for the Turkish bath. It was over a smoke in the pleasant lassitude of the drying-room that I have found him less reticent and more human than anywhere else'.

'The Musgrave Ritual', *The Memoirs of Sherlock Holmes* (George Newnes, 1894), and Episode XVIII in the *Strand Magazine* 'Adventures of Sherlock Holmes', is among the best-loved of all the stories and – unusually – narrated by Sherlock Holmes himself, but as one affectionate critic, M. W. Tooley, put it back in 1980, 'Unfortunately it is also one of the richest depositories of strange anomalies and questionable clues. The more we investigate the details and circumstances the more inexplicable they become.' Could it have been Holmes's recounting which led to so many anomalies and questionable clues? By contrast, aficionados rate *The Boscombe Valley Mystery* highly because of the way Conan Doyle builds up the character of the murderer so completely.

'The Boscombe Valley Mystery', *The Adventures of Sherlock Holmes* (George Newnes, 1892), and Episode IV in the *Strand Magazine* 'Adventures of Sherlock Holmes'.

The Hound of the Baskervilles (George Newnes, 1902). Originally serialised in the *Strand Magazine* from August 1901 to April 1902, it is set largely on Dartmoor in Devon, in England's West Country and tells the story of an attempted murder inspired by the legend of a fearsome, diabolical hound. The third of Conan Doyle's four Sherlock Holmes novels, it contains an arresting comment by a James Mortimer M.R.C.S., a House-surgeon at Charing Cross Hospital who brought the mysterious death of Sir Charles Baskerville to Holmes's attention. When Holmes solves the case, Mortimer says to him, 'You interest me very much, Mr. Holmes... A cast of your skull, sir, until the original is available'.

Acknowledgements

A singular pleasure in writing a novel is how people with great expertise will respond so positively to an author's request for information or advice. What camera (and more to the point, what plates?) would Watson have taken to the Reichenbach Falls in 1905? The answer came from Dr Michael Pritchard FRPS, the present-day Director-General of the Royal Photography Society. His expertise helped me construct the scene at the Reichenbach Falls where, like Moriarty fourteen years earlier, Watson's Sanderson Bellows camera and its precious dark slide tumbled over the edge into the roiling waters below. Or when Watson talks of his 'Service revolver', what calibre was it and what sort of ammo would he have used? Ask Mike Noble or Jeff Sobel (see below)…

What significant developments in crime detection were taking place in the Edwardian period? Ask Dr Judith Rowbotham who has played a great part in the detail of my plots. Until recently she held the post of Reader in Historical Criminal Justice Studies at Nottingham Trent University, resigning to continue her scholarship as a free-lance independent scholar and broadcaster (recent Time Team etc.), based in London. Her profound knowledge of Victorian history and Victorian print and periodicals is displayed in publications like *Crime News in Modern Britain: Press Reporting and Responsibility 1820-2010* (with Kim Stevenson and Samantha Pegg, 2013).

Further experts consulted include:-

Roger Johnson, Editor, *The Sherlock Holmes Journal*, for his unstinting help in checking (sometimes very) obscure facts. The publication *The Sherlock Holmes Miscellany* (History Press, 2012) by Roger Johnson and Jean Upton is a must for the world's millions of Holmes' aficionados.

Eric Shelmerdine M.A.B.I. W.A.D. General Secretary, The Association of British Investigators (ABI). He and the ABI produce an excellent journal.

Milica Pešić. Journalist by profession (she has reported for the BBC, Radio Free Europe, the Times HES, and TV Serbia), Milica has been ever-ready to provide me with translations and advice on Serbia and Serbian customs.

Barbara Wolff of Israel's magisterial Einstein-Archiv for her endless patience in responding to questions concerning Albert Einstein and Lieserl.

Professor Senta Troemel-Ploeetz whose deep belief I share in the much greater role played by Mileva Marić-Einstein than the jealous world of science yet recognises. See 'Mileva Einstein-Marić: The Woman Who Did Einstein's Mathematics.' Women's Studies International Forum, 13(5), 1990. Just as with the discovery of the molecular structure of DNA - the Double Helix – women's contribution to every field of humanity is too often deliberately overlooked, under-rated or derided, to the world's cost.

Jeff Sobel, for his counsel on weaponry. The son of my former UCLA Dean of Honours, Professor Eli Sobel, Jeff's knowledge of ancient and modern guns is exemplary. Jeff has just sent me a list of the armaments aboard the HMS *Dreadnought* when it was launched in early 1906, for my next Sherlock, set in Ottoman Empire times.

Mike Noble for his advice on the sort of heavy-game double rifles of the late-Victorian period Colonel Moran might have used.

Jack Reece QPM and Nicola Cox at The East Hastings Sea Angling Association for their invaluable assistance in providing period books on fishing (I myself not being an angler).

Howard White from St Leonard's On Sea, who drops by my home every so often and makes really valuable points on my latest plots as I relate them to him.

My description of the Reichenbach Falls is derived from and in admiration of the short essay *The Sherlock Holmes Trail – The Canonical Path To The Falls* written in 1948 by Anthony Howlett as a 24 year old Cambridge undergraduate (before he went on to become a founder of the Sherlock Holmes Society of London).

And most of all, to my beautiful partner of many adventurous years on four Continents, Lesley Julia Abdela. She is alongside at every step as a novel goes from inkling to final shape and on to the brilliant Steve Emecz at MX Publishing.

Some Recommended Publications

The Best of the Sherlock Holmes Journal, ed. Nicholas Utechin, Vol. 1 (Sherlock Holmes Society of London, 2006).

The Best of the Sherlock Holmes Journal, ed. Nicholas Utechin, Vol. 2 (Sherlock Holmes Society of London, 2011). See particularly the following excellent chapters: Nick Utechin, 'The Supreme Struggle' and Guy Warrack, 'Disguises In Baker Street'.

Crime News in Modern Britain: Press Reporting and Responsibility, 1820-2010 by Dr Judith Rowbotham, Dr Kim Stevenson and Dr Samantha Pegg (October 2013), for comment on newspaper reading contents and the habits of readers.

Max Beerhohm, *Zuleika Dobson or an Oxford Love Story* (London, 1911). Atmospheric tongue-in-cheek days of *Illi Almae Matri*.

H.W. Bell (ed.), *Baker-Street Studies*, (Constable and Co., 1934). See especially the Introduction by Bell.

James O'Brien, *The Scientific Sherlock Holmes*, (Oxford University Press, 2013). James O'Brien is Distinguished Professor Emeritus at Missouri State University. First-rate story connecting Holmes's vegetable poisons with concepts in botany, his use of fingerprinting with forensic science, and carbon monoxide poisoning and haemoglobin tests with concepts in chemistry. No science student or the scientifically-minded should be without it.

Nick Cardillo for his authoritative blogspot 'The Consulting Detective' at http://the-consulting-detective.blogspot.co.uk/

Michael and Mollie Hardwick, *The Sherlock Holmes Companion*, (John Murray, 1962).

Vincent Starrett, *221B: Studies in Sherlock Holmes*, (Macmillan, 1940).

Christopher Redmond, *Sherlock Holmes Handbook*, 2nd Edition (Dundurn Press, 2009).

Edgar W. Smith (ed.), *Profile by Gaslight*, (Simon and Schuster, 1944).

Maria Konnikova, *Mastermind: How to Think Like Sherlock Holmes*, (Canongate, 2013).

Gideon Haigh, *On Warne*, (Simon and Schuster, 2012). It was when reading this account of the Australian leg-spin bowler Shane Warne that the idea came to me that Holmes may well have been a leg-spin bowler at university and brought this skill – mental as much as physical – through to his work as a Consulting Detective.

Vernon Randell, *The London Nights of Belsize*, (John Lane, 1917), especially pp.147-57; a curious chapter where a character seems to echo Holmes's deductive methods. Watson would not like it: Belsize refers to him as 'that stupid practitioner'.

E. Chivers Davies, *Tales of Serbian Life*, (Harrap and Co., 1919).

Mary Edith Durham, *Through the Land of the Serb*, (Edward Arnold, 1904). The picture she paints of a priest and a cave church in a wild landscape is so evocative I have taken the liberty of using very similar words.

Mary Edith Durham, *Albania and the Albanians, Selected Articles and Letters 1903-1944*, ed. Bejtullah Destani, (Centre for Albanian Studies, 2001).

Michele Zackheim, *Einstein's Daughter: the search for Lieserl*, (Riverhead Books, 1999). An engaging detective story in itself and a most valuable research source by an intrepid American author. Her opening sentence is 'The search for Lieserl began in an old, gray cardboard shoe box. In that box...'. The author brings out the extraordinary nature of Serbian social life where reality and wishful thinking are often bafflingly confused.

Albert Einstein, Mileva Maric: The Love Letters. Edited by Jürgen Renn & Robert Schulmann, translated by Shawn Smith. Princeton University Press. Paperback 2001.

Eileen Blumenthal, *Puppetry: A World History*, (Abrams, 2005). A beautiful and illuminating 'coffee-table' book, starting with 'the origin of species'.

James Brown, *The Life And Times of Albert Einstein*, (Parragon, 1994), a recommended starter book on Einstein and easily read.

Nick Cardillo for his valuable critique of *'Einstein's Daughter'* at http://the-consulting-detective.blogspot.com/2014/03/review-holmes-and-mystery-of-einstein.html

Finally, Wikipedia. I have used the term 'magical' for the equation $E=MC^2$. For all who use Wikipedia extensively we would use the same word for that great source of information too.

Also from Tim Symonds

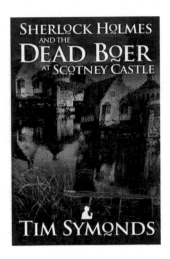

Sherlock Holmes and The Dead Boer At Scotney Castle

In 'Sherlock Holmes and The Dead Boer at Scotney Castle' the great consulting detective comes up against the rich and powerful Kipling League. Dr Watson recounts the extraordinary events which took place on a spacious early summer day in the Sussex and Kent countryside in 1904. None of the earlier stories chronicling the adventures of Sherlock Holmes compares to the strange circumstances which determined Watson to take up his pen to relate this extraordinary adventure against Holmes' express wishes.

Also From Tim Symonds

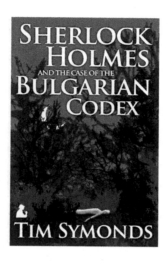

Sherlock Holmes and The Case of The Bulgarian Codex

It's the year 1900. Sherlock Holmes and Dr. Watson receive an urgent commission from the Prince Regnant of Bulgaria to come to Sofia. The Codex Zographensis, the most ancient and most sacred manuscript in the Old Bulgarian language has been stolen. Its disappearance could lead to the outbreak of war between Russia, Austro-Hungary and the Ottomans, three ageing empires disintegrating like great suns on every side of the Balkans. What follows is an extraordinary story of duplicity, murder, vampires and greed for vast estates in Bulgaria and Hungary, with the fate of millions in Sherlock Holmes' hands.

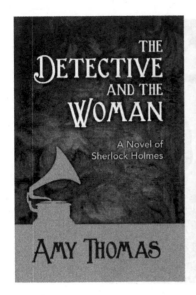 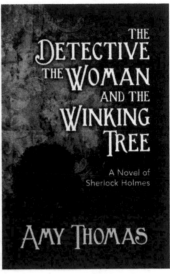

Also from MX Publishing

Benedict Cumberbatch In Transition

This performance biography is an analysis of a man in transition from working actor to multimedia star, as well as the balance between actor and celebrity. It looks at what makes this actor so well suited to play one of popular culture's iconic characters, Sherlock Holmes, and how Sherlock is so well suited to propel Cumberbatch toward greater global fame.

www.mxpublishing.com

Also from MX Publishing

Our bestselling short story collections 'Lost Stories of Sherlock Holmes', 'The Outstanding Mysteries of Sherlock Holmes', 'Untold Adventures of Sherlock Holmes' (and the sequel 'Studies in Legacy') and 'Sherlock Holmes in Pursuit'.

London, 1920: Boston-bred Enoch Hale, working as a reporter for the Central Press Syndicate, arrives on the scene shortly after a music hall escape artist is found hanging from the ceiling in his dressing room. What at first appears to be a suicide turns out to be murder . . .

Also from MX Publishing

  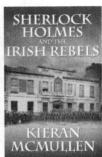

Three historical thrillers from the world's leading Sherlock Holmes military writer.

"Exciting, and full of authentic military detail"

The Sherlock Holmes Society of London.

Also from MX Publishing

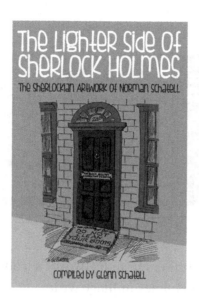

The Lighter Side of Sherlock Holmes

In paperback and hardback, 300 wonderful Holmes cartoons.

Also from MX Publishing

A Study in Regret

What if two had perished at Reichenbach Falls? One simple, disastrous error throws Sherlock Holmes from his intended Hiatus into a tortuous journey of sorrow and remorse. Far from home, broken in body and spirit, the haunted detective fights to survive the single most tragic failure of his career - a fight he cannot win alone.

www.mxpublishing.com

Links

MX Publishing are proud to support the Save Undershaw campaign – the campaign to save and restore Sir Arthur Conan Doyle's former home. Undershaw is where he brought Sherlock Holmes back to life, and should be preserved for future generations of Holmes fans.

Save Undershaw   www.facebook.com/saveundershaw

Sherlockology   www.sherlockology.com

MX Publishing   www.mxpublishing.com

You can read more about Sir Arthur Conan Doyle and Undershaw in Alistair Duncan's book (share of royalties to the Undershaw Preservation Trust) – *An Entirely New Country* and in the amazing compilation Sherlock's Home – The Empty House (all royalties to the Trust).

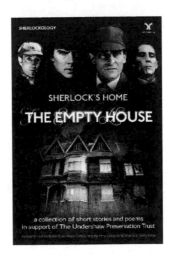

Amazon
9/8/17
14.95

Lightning Source UK Ltd.
Milton Keynes UK
UKOW06f2338290517
302274UK00001B/27/P